ARCANE KINGDOM ONLINE

BOOK ONE: THE CHOSEN

JAKOB TANNER

Dedicated:

To my mom and dad, who have encouraged and supported me in everything that I've done.

Special Thanks to:

Richard Sashigane for the awesome cover art.

Joseph Gisini for help with the cover typography and design.

Andrew Smith for sage advice.

All my family and friends.

Thanks to my beta readers and their amazing feedback:

Ailsa Bristow
Ezben Gerardo
Zach Goza
Jennifer Haviland
Jo Hoffacker
Ben Warren

This book wouldn't be what it is today without you guys!

1

It wasn't easy waiting to see if you'd live or die.

It was why the old man at the front of the line took his sweet precious time. He waddled forward, lifting his cane then placing it down again. Step by step. The echo of the cane on the terminal floor was like the ticking of a clock, each excruciating beat bringing me one second closer to my turn. My dance with fate.

The soldier managing the line barked through the air purifier tusks of his gas mask: "Hurry up or I'll throw you into quarantine."

The man stopped dawdling and stepped into the bioscan. He slouched his shoulders and muttered a quiet prayer to himself. A few seconds passed and a green light appeared above the machine, followed by a single shrill beep.

The passenger was free to go. The old man hurried away towards baggage claim.

The armed soldier yelled, "Next!" and the line shuffled forward.

Four people stood ahead of me. Four more turns until my own.

A little boy in front of me tugged at his mother's arm.

"I don't want to go through there mommy," he said. "Please."

The woman's face was pale and she had bags under her eyes. She gripped her son's hand tightly and said, "Shh. It will be over soon."

But the little boy was far from comforted: tears forming in his eyes.

I crouched down and smiled at the kid. "Why are you crying little guy?"

The boy sniffled and wiped his eyes. "Cause... I don't want to walk in there..."

"It's scary, huh?"

He nodded.

"But think about this: you had to go through the same scan before you got on the plane, didn't you?"

"Yeah..."

"And you must've been cleared—healthy as ever—otherwise you wouldn't have been allowed to even get on the plane, right?"

The boy nodded his head again.

"So do you really think you would've gotten sick between now and the last scan?"

"I don't know," said the kid.

"Well, did you eat the veggie option?"

The boy shook his head emphatically. Of course not.

I smiled at him. "Then you're fine."

The kid laughed, vindicated for his dislike of vegetables.

"You're almost through," I said, "Don't worry."

I stood back up and the woman smiled at me. "Your mother must be so proud of you."

I shrugged awkwardly, not wanting to disappoint her with the truth.

The guard ended our conversation abruptly, yelling, "Next!"

The woman bent down and kissed her son on the forehead. "Wait here and join me on the other side in a minute."

The woman walked through the two metal walls of the bioscan. The device scanned her body, searching for any signs of the virus. The machine buzzed and a green light flashed. The woman stepped forth onto the other side.

"Your turn buddy," I said to the kid.

He took a few hesitant steps before rushing between the detector's walls. As the scan commenced, the boy shivered. His whole body trembled. It was horrible to watch. The shrill beep went off and the green light flashed.

The boy ran to his mother, jumping into her arms. They hugged and kissed before grabbing their things and hurrying towards the exit. They had made it. They were free to enter the country. The boy turned around, smiled at me, and waved.

"Next!"

I stepped forward, passing between the two armed guards, and entered the scanner. The process was no different from going through a metal detector. The only thing you felt were your nerves. I stood there as the machine scanned my body for bacteria and deadly cells. I closed my eyes and counted the seconds. There was nothing to be worried about. Just as I had told the kid: I'd gone through the exact same scan only a few hours ago. Nothing had changed.

I waited for the beep. Silence. I lifted my head to see if a green light flashed. Nothing. I turned around to get confirmation from one of the guards. Instead I found an assault rifle pointed at my chest.

"Stay right where you are," said the guard from behind his gas mask. He had a rough voice with a slight country twang. "Don't move."

"What's going on?" I said. "This must be a mistake."

I whipped round and another guard was already there, semi-automatic ready in hand to blow my brains out.

"If you do not calm down, we'll be forced by law to subdue you."

I didn't move. I didn't open my mouth. Anything I did would be taken as a threat from these guys. All I wanted to do was elbow them in the face and run for it. But somehow I knew if I did, I would be begging them to shoot me.

The soldiers kept my head in their crosshairs. Army boots smacked against the floor, getting louder and louder. Security had sent out reinforcements.

Two new armed guards took position in front of the bioscan and started processing people.

The guard at my back patted me down and confiscated my phone, wallet, and passport.

"Hey! I need those—"

"Not where you're going," muttered the guard, patting me down.

Once finished, the other soldier said, "Follow me."

He spun around and marched forward. I stood still, frozen with fear. Paralyzed. What was about to happen? The guard behind dug the barrel of his gun deep into my skin. A sharp pain ripped across my back.

"Move it."

I caught up with the marching guard while the other one followed behind, making sure I didn't run for it. We entered a back stairwell and headed down the steps. A cold draft swept through. My teeth shivered and my shoulders shook. At the bottom was an open door, leading to the tarmac.

Waiting for us there amongst the airplanes and runways was a green army van, engine running. The guard opened the back door and climbed in. Behind me, the soldier kicked my back with his boot, knocking me into the van.

"What the hell?"

"Shut up," said the soldier, climbing in after me and shutting the door. He signaled the driver, "Take us to the quarantine facility."

I got up off the van's floor and sat down in the corner seat. "What are you guys planning to do to me? What exactly have I done?"

The guard who wasn't a complete dickhead turned to me and lifted his gloved hands to his head. He fiddled with his gas mask and pulled it off. The man behind the mask had a boxy head with a square jaw. He had a standard army buzz cut and blue stoic eyes. He blinked and a string of numbers and code fell along the side of his right eye. No wonder this guy didn't give a shit. He was an android.

"Passenger 1307-b," he said. "Clay Hopewell, aged twenty-four years old, citizen of United North America. Arriving from Charles de Gaulle airport, Paris, France. Flight number: 248. You've been put under immediate arrest for breaking international law by the decree of—"

"Breaking the law! How so?"

"Isn't it obvious, dumbass?" said the jerk guard, who kept his gas mask firmly on his head. "You got ZERO. You're a ticking time bomb now bud. I'm sure those French fucks are real happy with themselves for kicking out all the foreigners."

My arms shook, my shoulders shuddered. If what they said was true: I only had a few days to live.

"I was fine a few hours ago," I said. "How is this even possible?"

"You're asking the million-dollar question," said the guard.

We drove along an empty runway towards a large airplane hangar. Surrounding the perimeter of the building was a scaffolding of barbed wire, armed guards, sentry towers, and machine gun turrets. We slowed down at a parking gate. The driver poked his head out and spoke with another masked soldier. They exchanged a few words and then the barrier lifted. We drove on towards the hangar.

The army vehicle halted beneath the shadows of the large building.

"We're at your stop," said the jerk guard. "C'mon—out ya get."

He grabbed my jacket collar and dragged me out of the van. All the turrets from the different sentry towers pointed down at my section of the tarmac.

The guard led me over to a small shed-like building attached to the hangar. He punched in key commands and a metal door slid open.

"You enter the quarantine zone through here," said the guard. "We'll lock the door behind you."

"Is there a phone in there? How will my family be alerted of my whereabouts?"

The guard shook his head. "Don't worry. That's all been taken care of."

I clenched my fists and swallowed my anger. I brushed past him, heading into the quarantine zone.

"Okay," said the guard. "We'll open the next door after

we've sealed this first one. If you don't enter the hangar, we'll come in there and exterminate you."

He punched in the key commands again and the door slid closed, sealing me off from the outside.

The room was a cold concrete square. A metal door slid open, granting me entrance into the airport hangar. The open doorway revealed a pitch black room. The darkness was impenetrable. A stench wafted out from the hangar's entrance. It was like a mixture of rotten meat and shit combined. The smell made me not want to go any further. The guard's voice cut through my thoughts: *we'll exterminate you.* I lifted my t-shirt above my nose and stepped into the room.

The metal door slid closed behind me. The lights above flickered on and the sight was unbelievable. Horrible. This was the quarantine facility?

The floor was a sea of corpses. A few wrangled on the ground in their own vomit, moaning, but the majority of them were dead. In the furthest corner across the hangar was a heap of bodies, the mound like a pile of garbage at a scrapyard. Instead of rubber bags and broken bottles, there were bloated limbs and the occasional head, frozen in its last contorted gasp of life. They were empty husks, their skins saggy and hollow like deflated balloons. A snapshot of my future.

My stomach churned. I spun around and banged on the sliding door. "You have to let me out of here!"

I banged on the steel door with my fist until it was red and aching. "Fuck!"

I leant my head against the wall. What the hell am I going to do?

An odd gurgle echoed from behind. I turned around and scanned the bodies. "Is someone else in here? Hello?"

Emerging from behind the tent was a pale dismembered hand clenched between the mouth of a wrinkled old lady. The woman had long sweaty gray hair with patches of red blood stains. Her eyes were yellow and her nose was scrunched like a vicious wolf. She crouched on the ground, hunched and hobbled, her arms hanging between her legs. She dropped the limb from her mouth, swallowing back a piece of flesh. She pulled her dinner closer to her and growled at me.

"Trust me," I said. "I don't want any."

She growled louder this time and then barked. What was wrong with this woman? I got the sense she was telling me to get lost. To leave her to her tasty human limb. Fine by me. I stayed where I was, halfway across the hangar from her. But she didn't stop staring. She didn't blink. She growled and bared her teeth.

"I don't want any trouble," I said. "I'm going over this way. I'll leave you alone, if—"

She hissed, spit flinging from her teeth. She rushed towards me and jumped, fingernails out, ready to claw my face off. I lifted my foot and kicked her right in the stomach. She fell onto the pavement. She rolled over on the floor, got back up, and ran at me again. This time I kicked her in the head.

"Fuck off lady," I said.

I ran from the door. The woman's heavy panting encouraged me to run faster. I spun round and she was already halfway in the air, claws out. She dug her sharp nails into my shoulders and pushed me on the ground. Her sweaty blood drenched hair fell into my face along with her spit and bile. Drool dripped onto my cheeks as her lips opened wide for a big chomp of my flesh. I grabbed her neck and pushed her away.

She caught hold of my arm and pinned it to the floor. She did the same with the other. The woman's strength was overpowering. I kicked her, but she used her feet to keep my legs down. She had me trapped. Her hot breath poured down on my face. She licked her teeth with her tongue, readying herself for her fresh meal.

I was zombie chow-mein.

I closed my eyes, waiting to be eaten alive when a burst of machine gun fire echoed across the hangar. The deranged woman wailed in pain, shrieking. She collapsed onto my chest. Her body was sticky and warm. I pushed her off and scrambled to my feet.

What the hell was going on?

Back by the hangar entrance was a guard in a gas mask holding an assault rifle. I recognized his rough voice straightaway.

"Mr. Hopewell," said the guard. "Someone very important has alternative plans for your future."

2

"Alternative plans," I grumbled. "After you left me here to fucking die?"

I ran at him across the corpse-strewn floor, ready to body tackle him to the ground. When I got close enough to grab him, he spun on the heel of his rubber boots, and knocked my head with his elbow, bashing me to the floor. He grabbed my shirt collar and dragged me through the door back into the shed.

"You son of a—"

The soldier grabbed my wrist and twisted my arm. He paralyzed me in his grip. "We were following protocol. They'd send me in there if I refused to do my job."

He let go and I stumbled to the floor.

"Be happy you're out. I've never seen anyone sent in there come back."

I stood up and wiped the lingering zombie drool off my face with the collar of my shirt. "What the hell is going on? People aren't just dying of ZERO in there. Something worse is—"

"Preach it to someone else. I don't care. I'm following

orders. Now put that on." He pointed to a white plastic suit on the ground.

"What the—"

"It's a quarantine suit. Nothing you breathe in or out leaves that suit. It's an insurance policy. Now put it on."

I still wanted to punch this guy, but I did what he said. I picked up the suit, unzipped it, and stepped inside. It took me a moment to wiggle my legs through, but it worked. The soldier came up behind and zipped the back of the suit closed, including the air lock which kept my infected breath from spreading.

The soldier then pulled off his backpack and handed it to me. It was an oxygen tank with a bendable hose. It attached itself to the clear plastic face mask of my suit. I screwed it in and lifted my arms up at the guard.

"Happy?"

The guard grunted and spoke into a radio walkie-talkie. "All clear. Please open first door. Over."

The door slid open and we exited back onto the tarmac. The machine gun turrets aimed right where I stood.

"Good to see you again too," I muttered.

I followed the guard towards the parking gate. As we got closer something different came into view. A man in a tailored black suit and tie leaned against a silver BMW, taking a drag of a cigarette. His brown hair was combed back and he wore black sunglasses despite the fact it was a) night time and b) it made him look like a total douchebag. It was none other than my older brother William Hopewell.

He threw the cigarette on the floor and stubbed it out with his black leather brogues. He nodded at the guards and said, "Leave him with me. Thank you."

Next my older brother opened the door to his car and said, "C'mon Clay. We don't have anytime to waste."

BLACK ASPHALT ROLLED past as Will sped down the highway. He weaved in and out of traffic, cars honking as we passed them. He kept his eyes on the road, fixated on the city's glowing towers of neon in the far distance. The engine rumbled. The speedometer kept going up. I gripped the door handle for balance and peace of mind.

Will jerked the steering wheel to the right, cutting across the road, towards an exit lane.

"Where are we going?"

"Right now," said Will, hands gripped on the wheel, "We're taking a shortcut."

We drove off the highway and entered a part of the city I'd never been to. A neighborhood on the outskirts. Half the streetlamps didn't work and the others flickered on and off soon to be broken themselves. The road was littered with the broken glass of smashed storefront windows. The only items not stolen from these places were their "For Sale" signs. Graffiti adorned the walls of buildings. In deep red letters were the words: "THE END IS NOW."

Smoke billowed from a trashcan. A raccoon rushed across the street and I nearly jumped. I'd be a lot happier once we were out of this dilapidated neighborhood. Shadows moved behind the second story windows of nearby buildings.

"Are you sure this is a safe area to be in?" I asked.

Will stroked his hair and gritted his teeth. "We're fine."

We continued down the street, passing more fiery trashcans. Smoke enveloped the car, concealing the road ahead. Out of the clouds, figures appeared. Shadowy lumps. Hunched silhouettes. They stood in our way, blocking our passage. They moved towards us. They were scraggly homeless people, men and women, passing around a bottle of whisky. Their eyes were drooping and bloodshot. Most of them were missing teeth. One held a baseball bat. Another held a piece of wood with a rusty nail.

Will blasted the car horn.

They ignored him and gathered around the car. More figures joined the original gang, appearing out of the smoke and shadows. They pushed the car back and forth. Then a baseball bat came swinging at the window closest to me. I recoiled at the loud thump. The glass cracked. One more hit and it would disintegrate into tiny shards.

Will honked the horn.

"Fuck this."

He pulled the car into reverse and slammed on the gas. He knocked a whole crowd of people to the ground. He changed gears and drove at the scraggly rioters in front of us. They dove out of the way and we zoomed down the street.

A man in a ripped jean jacket ran after us with a green bottle, a flaming cloth dwindling at the neck of it.

"Step on it Will," I yelled.

The rioter screamed and threw the bottle in our direction. The bottle twirled in the air, flying towards the back trunk of the car. Will swerved and the bottle smashed inches away from us, erupting into a blast of flames.

Will kept his foot on the engine and we shot our way down the street. The wall of flames shrank behind us as we drove away. We turned onto a main road. One with working street lamps and other cars.

"Holy shit," I gasped. "Will—what the hell is going on? Where are you taking me?"

Will shook his head and wiped his eyes. "You know I

would do everything in my power to help you. You know that, right?"

I sighed and asked, "Are you telling me there's a secret cure for ZERO that only corporate big shots know about?"

Will shook his head and glanced down at his watch. "We're running out of time. There is no cure Clay. But there is a preventative measure. You may have already heard of it. Do you know the video game Arcane Kingdom?"

My eyebrows furrowed. I was surprised on multiple levels. Firstly, Will and I had spent entire holidays in our basement in the glow of the early Arcane Kingdom games. How had he forgotten? Our parents were very anti-video games, so we had to pool our allowances and cumulative birthday money to buy an out of date console older than we were and a copy of Arcane Kingdom 6. We only had enough for one controller, so I sat beside Will as he played the game. Even just watching, it had been mesmerizing.

The second reason for my surprise was my brother's current rescue plan was bat shit insane. Back in the day, the Arcane Kingdom franchise rivaled its competitors Final Fantasy and Dragon Quest. The series had been the hot new franchise *until*—thirty years ago—the creator and founder of TriCorp, Konrad Takashimi, announced the development of Arcane Kingdom Online. The new game promised to take the storytelling, adventure, and wondrousness of the classic single player series and connect people around the globe in a hyper-immersive virtual reality experience. The announcement came with much fanfare, but after a few years with no new developments, the game quickly disappeared from the public consciousness. A couple of decades later, it had been all but forgotten. The earlier titles in the series were spoken of with a quiet awe and fervor, but A.K.O. was now more of a myth than an actual game. People said the production had bankrupted the company while others believed Konrad Takashimi had secretly died. No one had seen the creator or his daughter Betina in years.

Everything changed last week when the company issued a press release stating those suffering from the ZERO virus were invited to upload their mind to A.K.O. and live a digitally reincarnated life online. All the retail VR capsule pods had sold out in minutes and the waiting list had already grown well into the millions.

"How did you even get your hands on the equipment?"

"Let's just say my company saw a great opportunity in investing in the TriCorp hardware. That's all I'm at liberty to say."

The BMW screeched to a halt outside the city's hospital. The parking lot was a mess of cars and shanty tents. EMTs weaved patients on stretchers through the crowd of vehicles and homeless refugees. Police managed the crowd, keeping the hysteria to a minimum.

The homeless campers gawked at me and my white quarantine suit. One woman ran up to us.

"Please... Help me... I'm dying out here..."

We quickened our pace and the woman gave up on us, running over to someone else to beg.

The inside of the hospital was as chaotic as outside. Nurses and doctors ran frantically in either direction. The phone rang and showed no signs of stopping. Will grabbed hold of a nurse by the arm.

"*Excuse me*," she said. "I don't know if you notice but I got a hospital to run."

"Sorry," said Will. "We're looking for the ZERO-TriCorp emergency wing."

The nurse sighed and said, "The TriCorp wing is in subbasement 2. Take the elevator over there."

We hurried over to the elevator. It was empty, offering us a brief respite from the hysteria of the rest of the hospital. Will scratched the back of his head and looked at his watch again. The way he was acting you'd think he was the one on the verge of death.

The doors slid open, revealing a quiet hallway, empty except for one woman sitting on a bench. My mother. She was her typical professorial self: hair tied tightly in a bun, thick black glasses, tweed suit with a matching skirt. Her heels clanged against the hospital floor as she came to hug me.

I embraced her and said, "I didn't know you were coming."

Her eyes were sad and melancholic. "Clay—it's good to see you. It's been—" She paused. "Too long."

"Where's dad?"

"He had a lecture," she said quickly and looked away.

I mustered a smile. Of course he did.

The three of us stood there in silence, basking in our awkward family reunion. As always, I was the odd one out. Between my brother dressed in his banker's business suit and my mother in her academic attire, I was clearly the one who didn't belong. Some things never changed.

A woman in a lab coat appeared from down the hall and walked towards us. She had red hair that fell past her shoulders and brown hazel eyes.

"Good evening," she said. "I assume you are the Hopewells." She turned to me in my quarantine suit. "And you must be Clay."

I nodded.

"Before we continue: I need you to sign a form agreeing to the operation we're about to do. So you understand how it works: the TriCorp headset connects nano-sized neural-cerebral transmitters to and from the user's brain, creating a simulation wave that adapts and envelops one's central nervous system and consciousness within the servers and data algorithms of Arcane Kingdom Online. You will do this from inside a glass containment pod full of psi-sensory liquid gel. This helps create deep immersion for the user. It also allows us to monitor your physical health from here in the hospital. The hope is we'll be able to keep your body alive long enough to complete the cognitive upload process which takes roughly forty-eight hours. I'm legally obligated to tell you twenty percent of user's who undergo this process do not survive. If you still wish to continue, please sign here."

She lifted up a holopad and showed me a long legal contract and a place to sign.

This was it. My one and only chance at survival. Will gave me a reassuring glance. Mom did the same. I wasn't ready to say goodbye to them. Or to this life. Or to this world. But what other choice was there? Shivering, I leaned in closely to the holopad and squiggled my finger across the air, committing myself to the process.

The doctor headed towards the swinging doors of the operation room. Before she left, she turned around and said, "Please step through here when you're ready."

Will hugged me tight. "Good luck little bro." He let go and wiped a tear from his eye. "It's your turn now. I hope you were paying attention in our basement."

I grinned. "I thought you had forgotten."

"Never. I was worried you had."

I shook my head. "No way. I'm still bitter at how much of the game you hogged to yourself."

Will and I hugged one last time and then I turned to

mom. She was as stoic as she'd always been. Her eyes were clear.

"Mom," I said. "I know you and dad didn't always agree with my life choices. Dropping out of college and—"

"It's fine," she said.

"Well I want you to know, even though we've spent all this time apart, I still—"

"I know. You don't have to say anything."

I sucked in air.

"Goodbye mom."

She nodded her head and I went down the hallway. As I pushed through the doors, my mother called out.

"Clay!"

I turned around. Tears filled her eyes and her lips quivered and all the words she wanted to say stumbled and disintegrated at the shivering border of her mouth.

The doctor placed her hands on my shoulder, urging me to come forward.

"Wait," my mother yelled, an exasperated croak echoing across the hospital hallway.

"Good luck," she said and swallowed a lump in her throat. She scratched her neck, clawing at where the words she struggled to express lay trapped. She wanted to say more—tell me all the things she and my father had never said to me growing up, like they believed in me and were proud of me and loved me—and maybe she was going to but right as she opened her mouth I was swept into the next room, never to see her again.

"We're running out of time Clay," said the doctor.

A sleek black containment pod with the TriCorp logo etched on it stood in the center of the room.

"If you will please unzip your suit and enter the chamber."

"But isn't it dangerous for you if I take off—"

She tilted her head in confusion. The doctor was an android. She didn't care.

I undid my suit.

"You'll have to take all your clothes off," the woman said. "Once naked please enter the pod."

I took off my clothes, shivering more and more with every layer I took off. Butt naked I walked over to the capsule and climbed into it. The doctor followed behind and placed the neuro-VR headset overtop my head. Next she closed the glass roof of the capsule.

"The procedure will begin shortly," said the doctor, clicking buttons on her holo-pad in the air.

A gelatinous purple liquid oozed into the capsule. This must be the sensory gel. After a few moments a voice spoke from the headset.

"*Hello Clay Hopewell. You are attempting a COMPLETE COGNITIVE UPLOAD into Arcane Kingdom Online. Before proceeding you must verbally accept the TriCorp terms and agreements as well as a legal waiver stating you are fully aware of the risks and consequences with COMPLETE IMMERSION uploading. Do you accept and agree?*"

I gulped. There was no turning back now. "Yes."

"*Are you ready to log-in to Arcane Kingdom Online?*"

I took a deep breath, nodded my head, and answered the prompt: "*I'm ready to log-in.*"

3

The capsule vibrated and shook. The sensory gel filled the pod. The voice prompt in the headset said, "*Entering Arcane Kingdom Online.*"

A powerful drowsiness overtook me; my eyes weighed with a great heaviness until I closed them shut and I fell into a deep sea of nothing. Then, like a snap of fingers, I was up above, lost in a gorgeous cerulean sky. I floated in the clouds without arms or legs or even a body. I was an ethereal being. Then I plunged, shooting through the clouds. Out of the puffs of air emerged a large continent floating in the sky. The land went on and on in every direction: mountains, forests, valleys. Water from streams fell from the continent and into the airy depths below.

Illyria once existed as a single landmass floating above the endless sea, said a scholarly and feminine voice in my head. *But thousands of years ago all of that changed...*

I flew closer to the landmass, zooming through snowy mountain peaks. The tall natural spires rumbled. Avalanches crashed down like wintry tidal waves. One mountain erupted with volcanic lava. The ground below cracked and separated. The land ripped apart from its very foundations. A family of elk were separated by the shifting landmasses. Towns and cities tore in two. Hundreds of people fell through the cracks and into the ocean of sky below.

The Great Rupture split the world into five continents, said the prompt as I floated through new scenes: I was on the edge of a landmass watching magical pirate airships be built by tiny fox-like creatures; next I was running through the forest with a group of rangers; then I was in a market square watching exotic goods be traded and exchanged for glimmering gold coins; rushing through the air I approached this incredible tower shooting upward into the sky like the needle of a rapier. *The floating world of Illyria would never be the same. Old alliances shattered and new ones emerged. What role will you take in the future of Illyria?*

I rode up the side of the tower and flew back into the beautiful blue sky. I went higher and higher, heading for the stars, the galaxy of this other world. I travelled through the cosmos: past shooting stars, meteors, and gorgeous nebulae until eventually I arrived at a black sea of nothing. The darkness dissolved and I was standing in a sandy desert under a misty sky. I was back in my body, clad in a light cloth shirt and shorts, no longer an invisible ethereal puff floating through the shifting historical landscape of Illyria. It was such an abrupt transition I fell to my knees, sinking into the desert sand.

I gasped at the twilight sky above me. I dug my hands into the sand and let it pour through my fingers. This wasn't like a video game at all. I stood up and ran over to a nearby oasis and kicked the water. It rippled and flew through the air before splashing back into the small pond. I bent down and splashed water on my face. It felt cool and refreshing on my skin. This was far beyond anything I expected. I lifted the palms of my hands: the detail and texture was amazing. Every crisscrossing line and wrinkle was there. A breeze ruffled my hair. A dry humid odor tickled my nostrils. I felt every single sensation. Wherever I was—Arcane Kingdom Online, Illyria, or digital purgatory—it was indistinguishable from the reality in which I had just come from.

The clear pool of water caught my reflection. It was enough to make me jump back in surprise. I cautiously stepped back and peered into the pond: my reflection hovered between the surface and the rocky sand below. It wasn't quite me. The image was partially myself: scruffy brown hair, green eyes, pale white skin from spending too much time inside reading comics and playing video games. There was even a brown dot, a birthmark I'd always had, lying underneath my right ear. Even *that* had survived the initial upload process to the game. But somehow I looked *better*, more in-shape, a handsomer, more idealized version of myself.

A window display appeared in front of me. The screen showed a full body image of myself with loads of customization prompts for changing my face, gender, race, and name.

So this was the character creation zone.

I examined the window display. Under the race tab I was currently classed as: "*Haeren (Arethkarian)*." Ah yes, the Haeren. All the previous Arcane Kingdom games had used that name to refer to the human equivalent race. I clicked on the button "*Haeren (Arethkarian)*" and a new window popped up.

Haeren
The Haeren are Illyria's youngest and most populous race. Their friendly nature and desire for travel—be it by

foot, carriage, or airship—has led them to creating towns and cities across the five continents. [All Haeren, except for Orensparon, have access to all professions and classes and start with a neutral to friendly stance with all other races].

More information followed about my specific sub-race:

Haeren (Arethkarian)

Arethkarians are known as the wealthiest and noblest of the five Haeren sub-races—that is, if you ask them. As citizens of the most populous and powerful continent Arethkar, Arethkarians believe themselves to be the true leaders of all Haeren people and Illyria as a whole. The lowliest beggar of their capital city Ryr's Ascension would lift his nose up at the most powerful noble of any of the other four continents. [Arethkarians start with a positive stance to all other Haeren sub-races, except for Laergardians for whom they share a neutral stance. Neutral with all other races].

Hmm. I did not like the sound of these Arethkarians. But I bet they came with an optimal starting position if nothing else. I recalled the awesome sky tower from the opening cinematic. That must've been their capital, Ryr's Ascension. It would be cool to explore. It was certainly worth considering. Though did I want to enter the world at its snobbiest focal point? Not so sure.

I clicked a button on the interface, *return to Haeren sub-races*. A new page appeared with the entire list of the different Haeren sub-races.

+Arethkarian

+*Laergardian*
+*Orensparon*
+*Renzarish*
+*Solmini*

Oh man. This was getting super complicated fast. Five sub-races! Plus there were all the other main races to contemplate as well. The depth and complexity of this game world was coming to life in these early choices. I clicked the Laergardian option, partly because they were the second choice on the list but also because, from the neutral stance mentioned before, they did not care for the Arethkarians very much which I took as a positive indication.

Haeren (Laergardian)
Laergardians are the Haeren citizens of the second largest floating continent in Illlyria, Laergard. The two landmasses are separated by the great cloud ocean, The Rift. Tensions between Laergard and Arethkar have always been strained as the the Laergardian Royal Family refuses to swear fealty to the Arethkarian High Council. [Laergardians have a neutral stance with all Haeren sub-races. Neutral with all other races].

Interesting. The Laergardians on paper were weaker than the Arethkarians in terms of racial bonuses, but it sounded like they had a more interesting starting position. World events would be centered around Laergard and such occurrences meant rare items and awesome loot drops. This was something to consider.

Curious about the other races, I pointed my finger in the air and pressed on the *"return to Haeren sub-races"* button which then let me press, "*return to playable races.*" A new list appeared in front of me.

+*Aeri*
+*Haeren*
+*Lirana*
+*Muumuu*
+*Rorn*

My mouth drooled at all the options. With some games I'd spend hours in character creation, experimenting with different builds and races. It was a whole game unto itself. But the harsh reality of my current situation was different. This wasn't a game for me anymore. I couldn't build a character, mess around with him, and then build another. No. This was the start of a new life. I only got one character, one chance to get it right.

I took a deep breath and started scrolling through the races. There were the dwarf-like Rorn: short, stout, and incredibly strong. Then there was the Lirana: a nomadic humanoid cat race specializing in both the merchant arts along with rogue and assassin classes. There was the tiny and adorable Muumuu: a fox-like race who were natural born healers and artisans. All of them were intriguing but none of them spoke out to me.

I clicked back to the starting menu in frustration. Only one main race remained. The Aeri. After clicking them I would have to make a decision and so far—I wasn't sure what I wanted. Would I simply settle and do the easiest option of Haeren?

I selected Aeri and felt myself get taller. My stomach sucked in on itself. My body slimmed out. My ears grew sharply angled and pointy. The color of my eyes turned violet. *Damn.* I was like a badass version of myself combined with Legolas.

Aeri

One of the oldest races of Illyria, the Aeri believe they are descendants of their mother tree, Gaia, in the Elder Woods. The Aeri are adept magic users. They are at one with the innate mana coursing through them and the mana within nature and all life. In the modern age, many Aeri have wandered from their forest and natural dwellings and have become great leaders, scholars, and politicians in greater Illyrian society. Despite this, many Aeri still tend to reside in their forest homeland and mini-mize their interaction with the other races of Illyria. [All Aeri get a +5 stat bonus to Spirit and Magic Attack Power. They start at a neutral alignment with all races except the Rorn which they begin at with a negative alignment].

I felt a flutter of excitement with these guys. I toggled through the four sub-races of the Aeri. The sub-races defined themselves with an affinity to certain elements. The Al-Hari prioritized air and water magic while the Murgain were obsessed with harnessing the power of fire. Interest-ingly the Chakren were fascinated by Earth magic and Crys-tallized mana, an interest which put them in a positive alignment with the Rorn race. But my favorite of the Aeri was the original sub-race I chose. The Eldra Aeri.

Aeri (Eldra)

There was once a time when all Aeri lived under the banner of Eldra. The Eldra believe in the Gaia Tree and the spirit of all things coursing through the world, connecting us all. They don't seek to worship one element over the other but wish to harness the innate energy binding all life. [Eldra Aeri start with neutral alignment to all Aeri sub-races. Neutral with all other races except for Rorn in which they have a negative alignment].

So why was I digging this race so much? First off, I was like the athletic basketball player version of myself. Secondly, I really liked how they were big on magic. When I was younger, I always played easier tank classes like warrior or knight, but knowing I would have to spend the rest of my life in this game made me really want to play a more complicated class. A small part of me also thought of my father, the academic. He never forgave me for dropping out of college. Well, mages and wizards were the scholars of these games, the keepers of arcane truths and ancient texts. Pursuing such a path might make him proud—if I ever did see him again.

I was ready. I selected *Aeri (Eldra)* as my race choice.

I was going to be a motherfucking elf.

The scholarly voice from the cut scene spoke in my mind: *To enter Illyria please choose your name.*

I would stick with my name. I needed to keep a reminder of who I once was; especially if I transformed myself into a magical elf.

I spoke out loud, "Clay Hopewell."

Are you ready to enter the world of Illyria, Clay Hopewell the Eldra Aeri?

What about class selection? Didn't I get to choose whether I was a knight or spell caster or whatever?

Your class must be pursued and earned within the game.

Got it. You had to do a special quest to unlock a class.

Cool. Then I guess I was good to go. The telepathic voice asked me again if I was ready to enter Illyria. This time I said: "Bring it on."

Good luck, young traveller, let your adventures bring you hope and prosperity!

The desert realm erupted into a bright cloud of glittering dust and my vision swirled until there was nothing but darkness.

4

Something slithered on the ground. Something slimy dragging itself across dirt and grass. The rustle of leaves and branches gently tickled my ears. My eyes flickered open and I found myself on a wooden floor, lying right beside a nail covered in flakes of rust. To my right and left were two wooden panels and in front of me was a door with metal bars like a prison cell. Beyond the caged doors was the silhouette of a person. A caption appeared above his head: [Skren Bandit]. He was shrouded in a dark navy cloak, his legs outstretched over the glowing green back of a massive slug-like creature. It was a gigantic snail, enlarged to the scale of an elephant. The bandit controlled the creature with both his hands gripped on its two slime tentacles. The mollusk slithered forward across the forest floor, dragging its shell and the caravan along with it.

I reached out but instead jerked my shoulders awkwardly and fell to the floor. My hands were stuck. They were clasped together by a pair of handcuffs. I clenched my fists and forced my arms in opposite directions like a circus strong man. The metal dug deep marks in my skin. The sharp sting in my wrists seethed throughout my entire arm and I collapsed on my back, out of breath, giving up.

I crawled back from the cage door. So long as my captor didn't know I had awoken, it was an advantage in my favor. *Now I had to think.* There must be a way out of here. How about my inventory? As I contemplated the word inventory, a whole HUD (Head-Up Display) appeared in my vision, along with a message: *Cannot Access Inventory When Handcuffed.* In the top left hand corner of my vision were two bars: one red for my HP (health points) and underneath it a shorter blue bar for my MP (mana points). A square box flashed underneath the bars with an image of handcuffs.

> **Handcuffed (debuff):** *Cannot access inventory or engage in combat. Maybe next time, you'll stay out of trouble.*

Goddamn patronizing game. I literally just entered Illyria. I haven't even had a chance to do anything. The HUD faded from my vision.

I lifted my wrists and inspected the handcuffs. The chain was orange with rust. I eyed the steel bars of my cage. What would happen if I knocked my cuffs against the metal?

Luminescent stars shone down from the night sky onto the lush green foliage of the forest surrounding us. The shadows of gnarled tree branches rippled across the cage's bars and wooden floorboards. My captor remained hunched and shrouded behind his cloak, focused on piloting the snail down the forest path. He was distracted. Good.

I stood up and took a few steps back in the caravan. Then I ran and leapt forward flinging my wrists at the steel bar of the cage. It clanged loudly as I smashed my head against the bar. I fell backwards and cut myself against the wood.

My HP dropped by 3%. A new debuff box materialized under my status bars, right beside the handcuff symbol.

Splinter (debuff): HP regeneration slowed by 10%. If splinter is left unattended, 50% chance of developing an infection (Bacterial Infection: HP depletes by 1% every minute until the infection is removed). Time period before potential infection: 30 minutes.

Is this game for real? Splinter infection—are you fucking kidding me?

My captor turned around. He had dark red eyes, a brown furry face, and the whiskered snout of a rat. He bared his sharp yellow teeth, growling. Then, even more frighteningly, he spoke in a sick and scratchy voice.

"If you try to escape again, I'll gut you and feed you to my snail."

My captor turned around and continued directing the slug further down the path.

I gulped. The designers of this game were clearly sick psychopaths. I put my back to the rat creature and lifted my foot to inspect the splinter. My god. It was miniscule. Yet somehow it had the potential to kill me. I squirmed my cuffed hands close to it and squeezed the flesh of my foot, pushing the wooden speck out through the tiny tear in my skin. I squeezed and pinched my foot and eventually the wooden speck pathetically poked itself out. I fell back in exhaustion.

You have learned a new survival skill: First Aid (Level 1)
When far from the comfort of doctors and healers, some-

times you need to aid yourself. Tending to your wounds
will increase this survival skill and open up new methods
for you to stay alive while on your own.

Great. Now I needed to figure out an escape plan. My
only option currently was to wait until we arrived at wherever this rat creature was taking me. A new setting might
offer more opportunities of escape. I leaned my head
against the wall and rested my eyes. An odd noise came
from behind me. A cough. I turned around and glimpsed
deep into the shadows of the caravan. A pair of bright silver
eyes blinked and glowed out from the darkness.

I wasn't the only prisoner in this cage.

5

I stared at the back of the caravan and whispered, "Who's back there?"

A soft chuckle emanated from the darkness. Starlight fell through the bars and I caught an illuminated glimpse of the passenger in the back. It was a Lirana male with cat ears poking out from his shaggy dark blue hair. He had a tanned face with big silver eyes and whiskers poking out from his cheeks. He wore a white tunic with a black vest overtop. On his legs he wore puffy black breeches and tall leather boots. Compared to my cloth attire and complete lack of footwear, this guy was a total aristocrat. Despite our differences in appearance though, the gentleman's wrists were cuffed like mine.

"You're far away from home young Aeri," said the Lirana with a mischievous grin. The man's long blue tail curled up and scratched his neck. "How ever did you end up here?"

I winced at my fellow prisoner. Was this guy for real? I wasn't sure whether he was a non-player character (NPC) or an actual gamer extra jazzed about roleplaying. I didn't receive any prompts in my HUD.

"How about you tell me why *you're* here?"

The Lirana was taken aback. "You certainly are coy. But I don't mind telling you how I ended up in this god forsaken caravan." He leant his head against the wall and scratched his chin. "I was playing a bit of cards at a pub in Claren's Crossing, you see. I was on a hot streak. Really raking in the coins. Until that rat bastard over there and his pals started cheating. Then it became a game of who cheats better and trust me—I'm good at that game. When I'd soaked them for all their coins, I wished them a good night and went on my way. But halfway back to the inn where I was staying, I got ambushed. Four rusty rapiers pointed at my neck." He shook his head, disappointed for not escaping the attack. "I can't really recall what happened after. The next thing I remember I woke up here with these cuffs on my wrist."

"Do you know where we're being taken?"

"Since we're talking about the Skren here, my best guess is they're taking us to their cave hideout where we'll be slowly tortured to death. Most likely over a roasting pit of fire. After that they'll eat us for dinner."

I looked at the man in horror.

"*Relax*—we'll be dead by the time they eat us."

We turned off the forest path and entered a torch lit cavern between two massive rock formations. As the Lirana had predicted, we were heading to a cave hideout.

Our caravan went deep into the cavern. The rock walls were orange beneath the glare of a great fire. Heat filled the air. Ash flickered. Wood crackled. The mollusk descended a large platform, revealing the Skren dwelling: a shanty town made of scrap metal, rotting wood, and tunnels dug through the rock.

A wailing scream echoed through the cavern. The

shadows on the rocks revealed a silhouette of a blazing fire and the black contours of a squirming Haeren woman, hanging from a spit held above the flames. She screeched and wrangled as the fire burned her alive. The Skren poked at her with their spears like chefs at a grill house, making sure her whole body got roasted properly. They wanted her skin crisp and golden.

I turned to the Lirana.

"Hey now—don't be giving me that scared look," said the cat man. "You're making me nervous. Listen—" He glanced back and forth cautiously and then leaned his head to me and whispered, "It won't be easy but the two of us could break out of here. What do you say?"

A new window appeared in my HUD:

New Quest Alert: Escape The Bandits!
Join forces with your fellow prisoner and escape the Skren bandits.
Quest Type: Unique
Quest Difficulty: Moderate
Reward: Freedom + 100 EXP
Accept: Yes/No ?

There really was no question, I wanted to get out of here quest or no quest. I accepted the mission, thinking *yes* in my head. The window closed in my HUD and the Lirana prisoner smiled at me.

"I knew I could count on you." He stuck out his hand and said, "The name's Shade by the way. No middle name. No last name. I keep it neat and simple. *Shade.*"

A message popped up in my HUD: *Shade has joined your party.* Underneath my status bars and debuff icons, a picture of Shade's face appeared.

"What are we going to do about these?" I said, raising my chained wrists.

Shade put his finger to his lips. "Wait."

The Skren bandit had disappeared. The cave walls outside angled upwards. The Skren were lowering us off the giant snail. I lost my balance and fell to the back of the cage. Next the caravan thumped flat onto the ground. The thick amber shell covered the cage door. The snail slid forward, dragging the shell through the dirt. The firelight of the caverns crept back into our cage. Two Skren bandits poked the snail with their weapons while a third pulled a collared rope and led the mollusk to a wooden stable where they closed and locked it behind a gate. Its tentacles poked through the fence, its bulbous eyes peering into the cavern. It was imprisoned like us. My sympathy waned though when one guard held out a dismembered hand, the flesh quickly disappearing down the slug's neck.

After feeding the snail, the two Skren returned to our now immobile carriage and stood in front of the entrance, keeping guard. The scraggly bipedal rats wore leather vests and shorts and had rusty swords hanging from their belts made of string. As I focused on them, more information than I expected appeared under the [Skren Bandit] caption.

Skren Bandit
Level 5
HP: 380
MP: 8

380 HP! Level 5 too. We were so dead. I called up my HUD and noticed a flashing buff under Shade's status bars.

Feline Vision (Passive Racial Ability) (Level 4): *The*

senses of a cat are strong in you. You can know your enemies sometimes better than they know themselves. Reveal the level, HP, and MP of all enemies eight levels above or below you.

Wicked ability and because we were in a party now I got the benefit of the information as well.

Shade brushed past me and headed towards the front of the caravan. "Oi! You guys really going to eat me because I beat you lot in a game of cards?"

The guards turned to Shade. Their snouts wrinkled with hostility. "Shut up prisoner. You'll be feeding our clan soon enough."

"I'd be careful what you do now," Shade replied. "You wouldn't want any visits from angry Lirana now would you?"

One of the guards stuck his snout through the bars. "I'd shut your mouth now kitty cat."

What the hell was Shade doing?

"Consider it shut," said Shade, running his fingers across his lips as if he were zipping them closed. He returned to the back of the caravan.

"Was that your master plan?" I asked. "Piss them off?"

Shade smiled and shook his head. He then lifted up his tail. Hanging from the tip of his furry rear end was a silver pair of keys.

6

Shade fiddled with the keys and undid his hand cuffs. Then he unlocked my wrists and the debuff icon disappeared. The cat thief grinned and said, "Now give me a hand with killing these stinking rats."

The Lirana crouched and said, "Follow my lead."

He crept over to the front of the caravan and silently unlocked the gate, escaping the notice of the guards. A new buff appeared on Shade's status bar.

Stealth (Buff): Stay hidden in the shadows, silent in the dark, unnoticed even in the open. 0.5% x LUCK your actions go unnoticed by your enemies.

The buff icon disappeared as Shade kicked open the door and punched
one guard in the face. The Skren growled and screeched. Its red health bar fell by a sliver, going down to 375/380 HP. The pitiable damage did not make the guard appear any less pissed off.

The rat bandit pulled out its rusty sword and swung it

towards Shade. The thief jumped out of its way. The bandit slashed his sword in all directions. Shade dodged and rolled around the incoming swipes. He leapt forward and delivered a punch to the bandit's stomach.

The caravan door swung open. A Skren guard rushed into the wooden carriage and unsheathed his sword. The creature panted with an excitement to fight, a hunger for blood. Its pink tongue lolled out of its mouth, resting over its large cracked yellow teeth.

It was now or never.

I squeezed my hands into fists and ran at the Skren. It took a step back surprised by my sudden burst of energy. I aimed my punch for the head, guessing it was the critical spot. My fist slammed into its skull.

Blocked!

What!? The Skren shook its head, more surprised by my weakness than any actual pain. His head was unprotected, yet the creature was so much stronger than me my hit was automatically blocked. The bandit didn't waste anymore time and slashed its sword at me. The blade swung through the air and dug through the skin of my upper arm. Bits of blood-soaked flesh flew across the caravan.

A hot pain coursed through my arm. My HUD showed my health bar drop by a quarter: 17 damage taking my HP down to 78. My heart raced. My breathing was frantic. My vision blurred. Shock overtook me. The pain in my arm was too intense.

Bleeding (medium) (debuff): *You have an open wound. You will lose 3 HP every thirty seconds. You cannot regenerate health until you stop bleeding.*

The bandit swung its sword again. I fell back and avoided the hit. I had to do something quick. The pain in my arm pulsed. Blood spurted from the wound. I frantically searched the caravan for something to fight with. Anything. To the left of me were our old rusty handcuffs. I grabbed them and my HUD prompted me:

New Item Alert! Old Rusty Handcuffs (ATKP: 3-4. Durability 4/10)
Do you wish to equip (Yes/No)?

Yes, I thought and gripped one of the cuffs. This was truly pathetic but this was life or death now. I spun around and slashed the air with the handcuffs. The Skren jumped back and then crept towards me again. It was overly cautious for someone kicking my ass.

I picked up the other pair of handcuffs and duel-wielded them like nunchucks. I ran at the Skren, completely freaking it out, and threw a barrage of metal blows at the creature's head, arms, and legs. I closed my eyes and swung like a mad man. It held up its sword to block me and a few *blocked* and *missed* alerts flew by in my retina display. But I kept going. I'd keep swinging until this unforgiving game debuffed me with lung cancer for being out of breath. Bring it on. I wanted to survive. I whipped the metal cuffs against the Skren's arm shielding his face. As I swung, the creature's health bar barely diminished. It was now at 369/380 HP. After all those hits—somewhere between twenty and thirty blows—I'd only dealt 11 damage.

The Skren bandit stopped cowering, thrusting his sword right into my stomach.

Critical hit!

The rat bandit wrenched its blade out of my gut, leaving a hole the size of a water faucet. Dark crimson blood leaked out of me. The blow did 28 damage. My health bar fell below fifty percent. I dropped the nunchuck handcuffs to the floor in shock. Next I fell to the ground. The pain overwhelmed me.

Bleeding (heavy) (debuff): You have an open wound. You will lose 3 HP every ten seconds. You can not regenerate health until you stop bleeding.

Even if I didn't take anymore hits from the bandit's sword I would be dead in under three minutes now. My vision was blurring. My cloth shirt was soaked in red. Blood leaked from my body, draining through the hole in my stomach.

The bandit approached me with its sword, now dripping with the blood of my intestines. Only two more hits from the sword and I was a goner. In the corner I noticed a loose nail lying on the ground. I reached out for it.

New Item Alert! Metal Nail (ATKP: Depends whether you have a hammer. Durability 8/10)
Do you wish to equip (Yes/No)?

I gripped the nail and thought *yes, this is my last goddamn hope.*

I rolled onto my side and cranked my arm back and thrusted my hand forward, releasing the metal nail like a dart. The nail flew through the air and—

Critical hit!

The nail rammed straight into the Skren's left eyeball. 20 HP slid off the creature's health bar. The Skren's arms flailed as he tried to pull the wedged nail from his eye socket. Blood leaked out from the wound.

I rose up and hurried over to the bandit. I punched it in the stomach and grabbed it by the head and wrenched out the nail and jabbed it back into the creature's bleeding eye socket. I did it twice more, landing two more critical hits.

The bandit screamed in pain. He grabbed hold of his sword and lunged the blade at the gaping hole of blood and guts that was my stomach.

I jumped but the blade touched the tip of my stomach wound, ripping more flesh off me. I tumbled back onto the caravan floor. I was down to 17 HP now. The Skren walked towards me ready to deliver the death blow. The nail remained lodged in its head where its eyeball used to be. It was no use to me there. But hell even with all my critical hits, I still hadn't gotten it below half of its health. What would one more shot to the eye do?

The bandit loomed over my cowering and defeated body. It lifted up its sword with both hands, ready to lunge the blade for the final blow. The sword came down towards me. I lifted my hand to protect myself.

A bright light burst forth and filled the room.

7

A ball of bright golden energy formed outside the palm of my hand. The power coursed from my chest and down through my arm and veins to the focal point of my palm. The ball of light shot from my hand. It burst forth and knocked the Skren bandit right in the stomach. The blast left a burn mark on the rat's skin and then dissipated in the air. The bandit stumbled back a few steps. Its HP bar dropped by 20 points; now at 278/380.

A new window appeared in my HUD.

Innate Racial Ability Unlocked: *Energy Ball (Level One)*
Manipulate the mana coursing inside of you into a ball of energy to damage your foes.
Skill Type: Spell
MTKP: 7-10
MP Cost: 5

The bandit charged at me with its sword raised. I lifted my hand again and—with a sliver of determination—seized the energy coursing in my arm and created a ball of light and launched it at the attacking creature. He flew back, losing another 20 HP.

I only had 8 HP left and less than thirty seconds before the bleeding killed me. I threw out another blast at the creature and then another and another. I stretched my fingers and shot my palm in the direction of the bandit but nothing happened. I bent my elbow and stretched my arm out again, hoping to reignite the blast. Again: no energy ball. I was out of MP.

The creature picked itself off the ground and ran at me with its sword. This was it. There was nothing left to do. I would have to face death. I closed my eyes as the creature dug its sword into my chest—

I waited for the blade to rip through my intestines. I waited for the prompt telling me I was dead. But I didn't feel a thing. No pain. Nothing.

My body glowed with a bright golden hue; my open stomach wounds had miraculously resealed. All my debuffs were gone. I was completely healed. My HP and MP bars refilled to the max.

Congratulations you have leveled up!
You gain +4 HP
You gain +1 MP
You have (3) unused attribute points that can be applied
to any of your five base stats.

But how? The creature was still in front of me. I hadn't killed anything. The answer to the riddle came in the form of a blade slicing right through the neck of the Skren bandit standing in front of me.

Critical Hit!

The Skren bandit's health bar dropped to a sliver. Shade ripped out his sword and did three rapid thrusts to its chest. The rat toppled over in death.

+87.5 EXP!

"Holy shit," I panted.

Way too close a call. If Shade hadn't killed his bandit, triggering a level up with an automatic health replenishment, I would've been dead. Nothing I had done from stabbing it in the eye with an old nail to blasting it with badass Aeri magic had been enough to kill it. I would have to be careful with mobs (hostile mobile NPCs) too far above my level. I had been rewarded for it though; I had gained a level and was now only 25 experience points away from gaining another. Still, I'd rather gain levels grinding out against level one mobs than come an inch away from losing my life.

Shade looked back and forth in concern.

"It's not that I dislike hanging out in this caravan *but* I'd much *rather* we got the hell out of here. You know, before the rest of this rat gang notices we've killed two of their brethren. But that also doesn't preclude us from looting on the way. Nothing—and I mean nothing—should ever stop us from grabbing the loot. Be it a fire breathing dragon or the moral ambiguities around stealing from the elderly. That's my life philosophy anyway." He gestured to the dead bandit at our feet. "I'd pick up the sword over there if I were you. Throw on the vest as well. I doubt those cloth rags you're wearing are doing you any good."

I bent over the dead bandit and hesitated as I reached for the vest. The scraggly fur was now patched red with blood. The body was still warm. I had to lift the skinny rat arms up and wriggle the vest off the corpse.

New Item Alert! Rough leather vest (DEF: 7. Durability 6.5/10)
Do you wish to equip (Yes/No)?

I selected yes and the cloth shirt I'd been wearing disappeared from my body and was replaced by the rough leather vest. When I had picked it off the bandit, it had been way too small for me but the vest appeared to grow with its user. Computer game logic for the win. Next I pulled the shorts off of the creature, keeping my eyes away from its gross rat underpants.

New Item Alert! Rough leather shorts (DEF: 6. Durability 7/10)
Do you wish to equip (Yes/No)?

My old cloth pants dematerialized and were replaced by the Skren's rough leather shorts. They came with a belt already attached—no extra stats, but a nifty sheath for a sword. Next I pulled off the bandit's rough leather boots and equipped them for another +2 to my defense. Finally *footwear*; bye bye splinters. I was very pleased with the new bonuses the loot brought to my stats. This new equipment meant I'd be getting a +15 defense bonus, which was 8 points more than the crummy cloth starting gear. Not bad. After such a horrendous fight, I'd take every advantage available. I picked up the bandit's sword off the ground.

New Item Alert! Thin Rusty Rapier (ATKP: 8-12. Durability 7/10)
Do you wish to equip (Yes/No)?

I twisted the grip in my palm. The sword felt good in my hand.

"Let's go," I said.

Shade winced at me with suspicion. "There's definitely something not quite right with you but I can't put my finger on it. I'll let you know once I figure it out." He then looked at the dead bandit. "Are you not going to cut off its tail?"

"What?"

"Cut off its tail. You can sell it to a merchant for a couple of coins. If we ever get out of here."

I shrugged and bent over. I grabbed hold of the Skren tail and sawed it off from the top. It took a few seconds but it was easier than I expected.

New Item Alert! Skren Tail (x1)
Do you wish to add this to your inventory (Yes/No)?

I answered the prompt and the long rat tail pixelated and faded away until there was nothing in my arms anymore.

"Perfect. Let's leave this decaying pit of rat dung," said Shade. "Now follow my lead."

He crouched and I noticed the stealth buff appear under his status bar.

"Do as I do," whispered the thief. "Crouch so you're low to the ground. Walk on your toes with the quietest touch. Cling to the shadows."

I mimicked him and received a prompt for learning stealth. A special buff icon appeared alongside my status bar too now. We crept out of the caravan and poked our heads around the corner. The entire Skren encampment laid completely before us. At the center of the tall cavern was a big fire, the flames lighting the whole place in a warm orange glow. A metal spit hung over the fire with the charred remains of the Haeren woman. I grimaced at the sight.

There were guards assigned to watch and manage the fire pit. Others carried logs and tossed them into the flames and turned back to the lumberyard to get more fuel for the fire. A few sat on benches, drinking and socializing. A couple of Skren danced, their shadows crisscrossing the cavern walls. To the right, the cavern went even deeper. Bright balls of flame hung from a wire leading down a dim path. I made out a few Skren with goggles and pickaxes, hammering away, mining the rocks.

These rat creatures had their own tiny civilization with jobs and social customs. Families and friends. It made me think of the two Skren bandits we had slain. Did they have children and spouses waiting for them back at their burrows of corrugated metal? Had we just wrecked homes?

This freaking game. The developers had really wanted you to feel everything. Excitement, pain, even guilt.

Beyond the big communal fire pit was a large ramp made of scrap wood and metal. We had gone down it on the back of the snail on the way in. It was the only way out here.

"How are we going to get over there without being noticed?" I whispered.

"We need some kind of distraction," said Shade, wagging his blue tail excitedly.

A silver light glinted from the fallen bandit Shade had slain. I hurried over to it and scanned the body. Shade had emptied the creature of all of its loot except for one item.

New Item Alert! Stable Key
Do you wish to add this to your inventory (Yes/No)?

I picked the key up. The glowing green tentacles of the imprisoned slug perked up.

"Today's your lucky day friend." I put the key in the gate and unlocked it. "Feast on your masters!"

The slug pushed the door open and slid towards the center of the encampment. The mollusk loomed over the screaming Skren. The slug dipped its head, opening its mouth and slurping a guard down its throat without swallowing.

Shade and I didn't waste any more time. We crept around the caravan. We stuck to the shadows, hurrying across the black open space until we were covered by the lumber shed. From there, we approached the ramp from the opposite end. These Skren weren't half-bad architects even if they didn't choose the best material. Shade grabbed one of the wooden bracings and gave it a tug. It was firm. Next he jumped up and balanced himself on it. He then lifted himself onto the next. He peered back over his shoulder.

"Hurry—we don't have much time till they tame that slug and notice we're gone."

I shivered. I guess I didn't have much choice. I jumped onto the bracing, wobbled, and grabbed hold of the next one for balance. I held onto the corner column and lifted my foot onto the next bracing and then pulled my other leg up. I did this repeatedly until more than halfway my stomach lurched. The ground was far below where I hung. If I fell from here I would lose all my HP and die.

I pushed myself off the last bracing and dragged myself onto the top gravel floor. I stood up and crouched, going into stealth mode. Where was Shade? In the shadows of a few rocks, a pair of sharp silver eyes glowed out like two floating orbs in the darkness.

I hurried over to him and he put his hand on my shoulder. "We're almost there mate. We get through this last tunnel and we're home fr—"

Two Skren bandits hurried down the passage with sharp spears pointed directly at us. Worse, charging behind them was a large bulkier Skren with an eye patch and a large sword. The caption above him made me shiver.

[Skren Bandit Leader].

8

The Skren bandit leader ran towards us, gripping his two handed great sword, keeping the blade behind his head, ready to slash us once in range. The Skren were already scary but this guy was terrifying: he was three times the size of the other Skren we had seen. He had broad bulky shoulders and a hunched back. His arms were thick and muscular. He was unnatural even for a Skren. There was something grotesque about him. He had an eye patch over his right eye and one of his fangs was golden.

Skren Bandit Leader
Level 8
HP: 610
MP: 9

"So uhh," said Shade, scratching the back of his head. "If you have any good ideas now would be the time to speak up."

What? I had been following under his lead. As a thief, he specialized in heists and escapes but as for actual head to head combat, he didn't know what to do. *Time to put my gamer brain to the test.*

"Okay, let's stick together and take out the small guys first. One at a time," I said. "Once they're gone, we'll focus on the leader."

The Skren squad charged at us. We had mere seconds before their blades made contact with our flesh. I whipped out my arm, charging an energy ball in my hands. I threw it out towards one of the lesser bandits. The blast of bright mana knocked him in the chest, taking out 5% of its HP. The blast forced the bandit to stumble behind the others, disrupting their triangle formation.

"Die prisoners!" yelled the bandit leader. He swung his great iron sword, spinning on the floor in a circle. He caught enough wind his body took the shape of a sword tornado. He rippled across the ground towards us, covering ten meters within a second. Both Shade and I jumped to either side to dodge the whirl of the blade. The bandit leader crashed onto the ground and quickly jumped up, out of breath and disoriented. *Great,* the ability had a kickback time. *But right now the leader wasn't my focus. Now was the time to take out the annoying guards.*

"Go for the one behind," I yelled to Shade.

We ran around the middle guard towards the one I'd shot with the energy blast. A stab of pain came from my ribs as I took a jab from the other guard's spear. He clearly didn't like us ignoring him. But I kept my target. The weakened bandit cowered as Shade and I approached it from either side. It didn't know where to point the spear so it held the wooden staff close to its chest, near its heart full of fear. It cried out as Shade did a quick stab at the creature's chest, taking out a chunk of HP.

"Aim for the head," I said, gathering the energy to form

another ball. I fell into a crouch, gripped my charged up arm for aim and balance, and shot the energy blast right at the creature's head. The blast flew across the air and hit the rat in the chin, scraping across its face in an uppercut attack. Its jaw flew backwards until it was facing the ceiling. A tooth dislodged from the rat's mouth and went flying out into the cavern darkness.

Critical hit!

The creature's HP bar steadily depleted as Shade piled on attacks with his rusty sword, jabbing the creature in the stomach and ribs. Blood overflowed through the holes in the bandit's leather armor.

"Distract him," Shade panted. "I have an idea."

I charged up a big energy ball and shot it at the creature's face. The blast of light knocked back the creature's skull. Shade jumped forward, transforming into a hazy silhouette for about a millisecond, before reappearing right where he'd been standing. He now stood with his rusty sword in one hand and the Skren bandit's spear in the other. Shade had pulled off his *Steal* ability mid-battle, leaving our opponent unequipped. Amazing.

The bandit lifted his empty hands in horror. He was now defenseless. I pulled my sword out from its sheath. The bandit's eyes bulged in fear at the sight of my weapon. I gripped the handle and lunged forward at the dying Skren.

Something knocked into my back sending me skidding across the dirt. A horrible pain coursed through my entire body. My back stung. My HUD showed I had lost more than 50% HP. I spun around. The bandit leader was about to decapitate me with his massive sword. I rolled out of the way and scrambled to my feet. Both the bandit leader and his guard headed towards me with their weapons raised. I didn't like this two on one scenario. Not at all. Beyond my approaching enemies, Shade delivered the final death blow to our target Skren, yanking his blood drenched sword out of the dead bandit.

+87.5 EXP!

The ground at my feet glowed and all my aches, pains, and bruises disappeared. My HP and MP fully replenished.

Congratulations you have leveled up!
You gain +4 HP
You gain +1 MP
You have (3) unused attribute points that can be applied to any of your five base stats.

I closed the prompt on my HUD. I didn't have time to deal with distributing attribute points. I had a rat pack to kill.

The leader and his crony crept towards me. My drawn sword and magic hand made them weary of making any quick moves. There was no reason to rush; they would overtake me with force eventually.

Too bad they had forgotten about my friend.

Shade moved silently behind my attackers. When his shadow loomed over the smaller Skren guard, he jammed his sword into the creature's skull. Red blood sprayed onto Shade's whiskers and face. The rat bandit let out a horrible scream and Shade ripped the sword out of the creature's skull and then thrust the blade back in. Pieces of brain flew through the air.

Both the bandit leader and the dying guard turned to

attack Shade. I summoned an energy blast and shot it at the bandit leader this time. I hit the large rat in the shoulder and did a modest twenty hit points of damage. The creature returned its attention to me as Shade took on the dying bandit. The leader growled. It ran at me and then leapt in the air. Its shadow covered the ground at my feet. In the air, the creature held its sword back, the force of his jump added more and more energy and weight to the swing of his blade. If the sword hit me it would be an instant kill. I jumped out of the way as the bandit leader's sword crashed into the ground, a cloud of dirt bursting from the impact.

It took the leader a moment to recuperate. I returned my sights to the normal Skren bandit. I powered up an energy ball and shot it off at the back of the Skren's head.

Critical hit!

Shade did a quick jab at the creature's ribcage. He strafed to the side and did another jab. He then twirled behind—so quickly the Skren didn't have time to register what was going on—and did a final stab in the back. A fountain of crimson blood burst out the bandit as it toppled over onto the ground.

+87.5 EXP

The Skren leader let out a bellowing scream. It shook the cavern walls and small bits of rock fell from the ceiling. A coat of red energy swirled around the bandit leader. Shit —it must've entered a new powerful mode when its two minions were defeated.

The large rat creature sheathed his great sword behind his back and pulled out a rapier. In a flash of a second, he was right in front of me, the top of his sword coming straight for my face. I lifted my blade to block the attack. The rat's one yellow eye bulged and its snout rippled into an antagonistic growl. It pushed its sword against mine. As our blades clashed, the creature leant in and bit my shoulder. I kicked it in the chest and its teeth dragged through my skin. The creature stumbled backwards.

My shoulder burned with two red streaks of torn flesh. The bite had taken a quarter of my HP off. My body pulsed with pain and my vision darkened.

Poisoned (Debuff): You have been poisoned! You lose 2 HP per 3 seconds until poison wears off (Duration: 1 minute)

Yikes. 40 HP gone in a minute. I would be left with just over 30 HP. If I took a single hit from this thing I'd die. The shock of the poison ached through my entire body. My muscles and limbs tensed and throbbed from the pain.

Shade had lunged the sword into its ribs, shaving off another 20 damage on the rat leader. They danced with their swords. The clash and clang of metal echoed through the cavern as the cat man and rat bandit battled away with their blades.

"Watch out for its bite," I yelled. "It has poison fangs!"

"Gotcha," Shade replied, dodging an attack and rolling to the side. He lunged, shooting his sword forward. The bandit leader parried. He kept his back to me and I took the opportunity to power up an energy ball and shoot it at the back of his neck. The hit did 20 damage. The fur on his body struck out in pain.

The leader rolled away from us and sheathed his rapier. He then pulled out his great sword from behind him. "Prepare to die scum." He held the sword in front of him, holding the handle with two hands. He pointed the sword out to us and unleashed his spinning AOE attack. The whirl of blades rushed towards Shade, knocking him back and taking more than a third of his HP off. It ricocheted off Shade and flew towards me. I sprinted towards the shadows of the wall and crouched into stealth. The sword tornado bashed into a wall of rocks.

The bandit leader stood up, muddled and confused. Following the creature's super ability, his great sword had magically returned to its position slung on his back. His body stumbled in a dizzy stupor.

"Hey! Any chance you can steal the leader's great sword?" I said.

Shade shook his head. "Too big to steal mid-fight and I wouldn't be able to wield it anyway."

Damn, Thief class must not be able to wield heavy weapons.

"Okay—new idea. Try and steal the rapier before it wakes up, that way he won't be able to deal too much damage between AOE attacks."

Shade grinned. "You know you've come a long way since I met you five minutes ago."

He winked and ran ahead towards the dizzy bandit. He yanked it off the guy and the sword dematerialized into Shade's inventory. He jumped back and hacked away at the bandit leader, whittling away its health. I fired off another energy ball. The last one I'd be able to use in a while as I waited for my MP to regenerate.

The bandit leader was at less than half health when it returned to proper consciousness. It attempted to grab its rapier and stopped, confused at the fact it was missing from its sheath.

"Looking for something," laughed Shade, unleashing another attack at the creature.

The bandit leader growled and pulled out its great sword. He swung for Shade, delivering a bloody streak across his chest. I ran behind the creature and went for a stab attack. My blade sliced across the creature's back. I did a pitiable 5 damage. A pain pulsed through me, making my legs wobble. The poison made it difficult to think and aim properly.

The Skren turned towards me and swung his sword at my head. I jumped back and dodged the attack.

Shade ran up and slashed it in the back. It screeched in pain and rage.

The bandit cooled and gripped the sword with two hands and held it in front of him. Uh oh. He was preparing the AOE attack.

"Run!" I yelled and headed towards the cavern walls. If we triggered stealth in the shadows, the tornado targeting would be skewed and it wouldn't hit us. Victory was ours if we survived this next attack. All I had to do was not get hit. I darted for the walls and felt the gust of the sword tornado behind me. I strafed and strafed, barely outmaneuvering it. I was about to dodge it again when a burst of poison screwed up my footing and I twisted my leg, falling back. The sword tornado grazed me, skidding across my skin, taking out 30 HP.

Oh no.

My HP bar slid down to 18. The poison debuff would last another thirty more seconds. It would kill me, feast upon my dying flesh.

The bandit leader emerged from its AOE attack, stumbling and dizzy.

There was only one last hope now. I rushed the dazed

bandit leader and flung my arm forward, thrusting my sword at its undefended head. I took off a bunch of damage. Shade was right behind me slicing at its back. I grabbed the creature by the snout and jabbed my blade into its eye over and over.

Critical hit!
Critical hit!
Critical hit!
Critical hit!

I was at 6 HP now. I had three seconds. I kept jamming the sword into the creatures eye, generating critical hit after critical hit. C'mon, c'mon, c'mon. I had one second left. I wasn't going to make it. I went for one last stab. This was it.

Critical hit!

A horrible screech echoed through the room. A shower of lights filled my HUD. My HP and MP bars replenished as the prompts rolled in.

Congratulations you have leveled up!
You gain +4 HP
You gain +1 MP
You have (3) unused attribute points that can be applied to any of your five base stats.

9

"Time to go," said Shade.

Screams emanated from the encampment below. The Skren were still taming the giant mollusk.

I headed over to the dead rat bandits. I scanned their bodies and equipment, seeing if any of it was worth taking off them.

Skren Bandit
Rough Leather Vest (DEF: 7. Durability 6.5/10)
Rough Leather Shorts (DEF: 6. Durability 7/10)
Rough Leather Boots (DEF: 2. Durability 8/10)
Thin Rusty Rapier (ATKP: 8-12. Durability 7/10)

None of the stats were better than what I already had but the rapier and vest would catch me coin at a market somewhere. I opened my five-slot inventory and discarded the useless cloth starting gear and yanked off all of the Skren bandit's clothes. Along with the two rat tails (crafting materials and loot trophies stacked in your inventory) I'd be completely full. I'd have to buy a bag or an inventory increasing enchantment. Item management was always a pain in the ass otherwise.

Once I'd stripped the bandit, I kneeled over and cut off its tail and then let it dematerialize into my invisible inventory. I ran over to the other bandit and did the same. I eyed up its equipment but when I pulled off its boots, my inventory refused to take it. Equipment did not stack in your inventory like the rat tails did.

My greedy eyes turned to the dead bandit leader.

"Shall we?" I said to my companion.

"Even I know we should retreat to the woods," the thief sighed. "But you know me too well. The great sword will fetch a mighty price at the market. It would be a pity to leave it behind."

We walked over towards the bandit leader, soaking in its puddle of blood on the ground. We were two meters from it when its arm twitched. I grabbed Shade by the shoulder.

"Stop. Did you see that?"

"A newly born corpse does funny things," explained Shade, shrugging off my arm.

A burst of blood shot out of the rat leader's shoulder. A piece of bone burst forth as the skin of the corpse bubbled in odd contortions. The clawed finger of the creature dug into the ground, gripping it for balance. It pushed itself up right. The rat face was there but red fleshy tentacles oozed out of both of its eye sockets. The creature's skin shriveled and bulged.

"What is happening?"

Shade shook his head. "We need to run."

I scanned the creature but its information was disconcerting.

Skr3n B∧ndɪt L33der

Level ??
HP: ??
MP: ??

What the hell? Something wasn't right about this thing. It gurgled and burped and purple puss drooled out of its mouth.

"Shade?"

But the thief was already meters ahead of me, dashing away.

I turned to run but the demonic creature in front of me screeched. I was unable to move. What was happening?

Paralyzing fear (debuff): *You are so scared you are paralyzed (immobility duration: 1 minute)*

"Shade!" I yelled. "Come back. I can't move."

The creature waddled towards me. It lifted up its arms and pointed at me. Its arm stretched and mutated, turning into a tentacled pincer. It touched my right arm and my whole HUD went deep red.

Instant kill!
You are dead!

10

I woke up. My eyes bulged with terror. I scrambled to my feet.

Whatever just happened to me—there were no words to properly describe it. It was like I had existed in eternal nothingness for hours, days, possibly even years. It was what solitary confinement did to you: it messed up your sense of time, order, and reality. My stomach wrenched. I knew no amount of therapy would ever let me forget what it was like to die. I wouldn't wish it on my worst enemy. To exist in a plane of reality where nothing was all, where there was only absence.

It was made worse by coming back to life. At the time I wasn't able to consciously think through the horror. Now the concept became worse and worse in my mind.

A prompt appeared in my HUD:

Quest Failed: Escape the Bandits!
You failed to escape the Skren bandit encampment
without dying. Better brush up on those stealth skills
rookie!

Damn. I failed my very first quest in this game. Not a promising start. I closed the prompt and took in the next one.

Death's Punishment (Debuff): You feel the horror and pain of death. You lose all EXP gained towards your next level. You gain 30% less EXP on kills (Duration: 6 hours). All ATKP and MTKP damage reduced by 10% (Duration: 6 hours). HP and MP regeneration 10% slower (Duration: 6 hours).

Brutal. The EXP loss wasn't too bad for me this time as I had just leveled up and had barely progressed towards my next but it would be a brutal blow to anyone at higher levels. Also the stat debuffs and EXP gain penalties were a real pain. The after effects of death were really meant to sting. The worst part so far was still the purgatory I'd been sent to. The great traumatic sea of nothing.

How long had I been out for?

I had respawned in the Skren cavern. I retained all my equipment and weapons. My body was intact: no bruises or scars. I examined my right wrist where the *thing* had touched me. It had left a mark: a swirling black circle with jagged edges. I waited expectantly for a prompt but nothing appeared. Ominous. I'd have to research into what this symbol meant. But for now, I had to get out of here.

The cavern was quiet. Smelly too. Puddles of blood lingered on the gravel ground from our battle with the bandits. The great glow of the fire had dwindled in the cavern below. I fell into stealth mode and hurried over to the ramp on the edge of the encampment.

I gagged in horror.

Bodies everywhere. Guts and organs laid strewn all

across the encampment. Around the fire, on the ramp, near the lumber mill. The mutant creature had massacred its own kind.

I turned around and ran out the cavern. I had to escape. I needed to find the nearest town. Warn them this creature was roaming the woods.

The cavern opened to a small encampment of tents. More dead Skren bodies laid strewn across the ground. I stepped over the corpses and headed towards the woods. The night sky was dark blue and clear. Stars stretched across the expanse of space like glittering dust. Two moons glowed down on the night, making it easy enough to see through the darkness of the trees.

I took a few steps into the forest when someone came crashing down from above. The force pinned me to the ground.

I elbowed whoever attacked me. I pushed off the ground and ran through the woods. I sprinted past thick ancient trees, hopping over the giant roots entangled in the forest floor.

Alive for ten minutes and already I'm running for my life again.

My heart pounded as I headed deeper into the shadowy woods. I had no idea where to go. I had to get away. My throat burned. I panted like a mad man. Don't stop. The goal was to keep moving. I headed towards a group of trees when a shadowy figure stepped out in front of me and into the glimmer of moonlight.

I recognized the man.

It was Shade.

He didn't recognize me though. He lifted his sword and pointed it at me.

"Shade—what's going on?"

The thief shook its head and hissed at me. "Don't play tricks with me foul creature. How do you know my name?"

"What do you mean? We fought a bunch of bandits—"

"You impersonate my fellow prisoner. I watched him die. Now you reincarnate yourself to appear as him like that bandit leader."

"No," I said, shaking my head. "Shade—it's me! We fought those bandits and then the leader, I don't know what happened to him. He changed and I died."

"And now you're back and possessed by a demon!"

"No I came back Shade," I said. "I came back to life. I can't explain it properly but I'm different from you. I don't come from here. Illyria isn't my original world."

Shade took a step back. His tail froze. He lowered his blade and sighed. "I guess the rumors are true then. The Chosen truly have returned."

"The Chosen?"

Shade nodded and scratched his hair. His tail wagged and he looked up to the two moons in the sky, whispering a prayer.

"All of the great religions speak of The Chosen in one way or another. The Lirana call them the *Akhen'a*, which means something close to 'those that return'. The Rorn have their own name for them and so do the Muumuu and Aeri. The Haeren believe themselves to be the true descendants of The Chosen. Stories of these beings have been around since forever. The main tale goes as follows: a long time ago before the Great Rupture, a group of beings saved Illyria from an evil destructive force. Afterwards they were never seen again. But, as the story goes, The Chosen were prophesied to return someday to rid Illyria of a new evil. The arrival of The Chosen isn't a blessing but an omen for a new dangerous age."

This was clever work on the devs part for incorporating players into the lore of the world. New approaching evil, however, did not sound as cool. Was the mutant Skren the new evil? Something told me it wasn't. There was something very *off* about the mutant Skren. From the way its name appeared in the caption to the strange way it killed me. I hid my right arm from Shade's view. I'd keep the mark to myself for now. At least until he grew comfortable with me again.

"What happened to you after I died?"

Shade shook his head. "I ran. I'm sorry for leaving you behind. But one look at that thing and I knew it would be a losing battle to fight it. I ran out here and tried to warn the Skren outpost guard but they wouldn't listen to me. They wanted to fight so I ran from them. I hurried into the woods and climbed up a tree. I hid up above in the branches and listened to all those Skren scream."

Shade wiped a tear from his eye.

"As much as I don't care for the Skren—it was tough to listen to their slaughter. The creature came out here, massacred the outpost and then rushed into the forest. I haven't heard or seen it since. I only came down when I finally spotted you running out of the cavern. I thought you were a lesser demon who might have answers for me. I'm sorry for threatening you."

I shook my head and waved my arms. "No worries man."

You have gained status with Shade. You have gone from "Stranger" to "Trusted Acquaintance."

"Listen to me, Clay. We need to get as far away from here as possible. I know someone at Claren's Crossing who can stow us away on an airship. What do you think?"

Shade wanted to run away. It wouldn't help our predica-

ment. Plus that mutant thing was still out there. We needed
to warn the nearby towns; make sure they were prepared
for it.

"Where's the nearest town? Let's head there. We need to
warn people about the mutant Skren."

"And be put behind bars for having our heads
possessed? Trust me, I've been in the village drunk tank
before and it is not a pretty place."

Appealing to Shade's sense of moral responsibility was
the wrong tactic. I switched gears. "Also—there are rewards
for bringing valuable information to the right authorities."

Shade's ears perked up. "Reward you say?" His tail
wagged and he scratched his chin. He was definitely imag-
ining a mountain of gold coins to swim in. "Any thief can
sell stolen goods, but real criminals trade in the most valuable of currencies: *information*."

New Quest Alert: Mystery Creature in the Woods
Report to local authorities about the S^%AD"@@@@@
in the woods. Speak to a member of the Royal Knights of
Laergard at their guild hall in Land's Shield or any of
their outposts (such as Arondale and Claren's Crossing)
Quest Type: Unique
Quest Difficulty: Moderate
Reward: 100 EXP + More Information
Accept: Yes/No ?

I paused. The quest itself was unable to even name the
creature we had fought. The game was malfunctioning. Or
attempting to make a quest around an issue its algorithms
didn't fully understand. It was strange. Accepting the quest,
however, was a good way of ensuring Shade stuck with me

and led me to the nearest town. I agreed to the quest and the prompt disappeared.

"Where's the closest town?"

"Arondale," sung Shade, excitedly. "Where the mead is sweet and the Haeren girls are even sweeter. Shall I lead the way?"

I nodded my head and walked a few paces behind the rogue as he led me deeper into the dark woods.

11

We walked in silence. I suffered through the pain of the death's punishment debuff while Shade focused on leading the way. Neither of us were in chatty moods. Not after the evening we'd had. Monsters peered out at us from the shadows. Their red eyes glowing through the darkness. They didn't attack us though. Maybe they knew we weren't in the mood for another fight.

Since accepting the quest, Shade and I were party members again. I took a moment to look over his stats. Like me he had leveled up while fighting the Skren.

Shade
Level 4
Race: Lirana
Class: Thief

HP: 137
MP: 11

ATKP: 21

MTKP: 3
TGH: 14
SPIRIT: 4
LUCK: 36

I closed Shade's stat page and contemplated my own. I had nine unused attribute points. I was thankful I hadn't lost them when I died. Games did that to you and it was terrible. You'd think with all the close calls that I would put points into Toughness but it didn't feel right. If I were going to be a magic user, I would have to accept partying up with a tank. I put all nine points into Magic Attack Power. I pulled up my new stats to take a peek.

Clay Hopewell
Level: 4
Race: Aeri (Eldra)
Class: N/A

HP: 107
MP: 28

ATKP: 3
MTKP: 29
TGH: 4
SPIRIT: 20
LUCK: 3

I half tripped over a mangled root and closed my HUD. We traversed the woods for another few minutes. The trees cleared and we approached a dip in the land and discovered a large valley of farms. There were corn and wheat fields, pig stys and chicken coops, and even a small apple orchard.

Small windmill houses dotted the farm landscape while a winding dirt road curved through the farms leading up to a bridge which crossed a rushing stream and revealed a small bustling city in the distance.

Smoke and eerie unnatural lights glowed from beyond the walls of the urban dwelling, a bright purple and green haze floating above in a hazy fog. Thick irrigation and sewage pipes stretched out from the walls like spider legs and ran through the valley towards a large river and lake. Where were we heading?

"Is this—"

"Yes it is," said Shade, ripping off a batch of red berries from a nearby bush and tossing them into his mouth one by one. He spoke with his mouth full: "Arondale."

We headed down the road between the farmer's fields. It was late, so the roads were quiet. We passed by quaint houses with thatched roofs. Lit candles on homely kitchen tables glowed out through mullioned windows. We passed by stables and parked wagons. The smell of horse and pig manure felt oddly comforting. It reminded me of field trips to hokey historical farmhouses my elementary school took my class on. The smell was a faint reminder of the world from which I had come from. Which shouldn't be a surprise. This whole reality was based on our world, shaped and distorted by the deranged programmers and developers over at TriCorp. Echoes of Earth in Illyria only made sense.

As we approached Arondale, the wall grew in size and stature, its shadow looming over us even from far away. To cross the stream towards the wall's gate, we walked over a bridge made of bright white stone. Lamp posts stood along the bridge, bright with a purple luminescence.

"What's powering these lamps?" I asked.

"You're a weird one, you know," said Shade. "I know the

Aeri generally don't care for manatech but c'mon, you know how mana crystals work. Tiny shards of purified mana, lasts ages, and can keep streets lit at night. Same principle for airships though you need more than a tiny shard for them. Expensive stuff, mana crystals. I know a guy who says he knows a guy who can get us to a mine full of purified mana. A few crystal shards would be enough to make you rich for life *but* it's for that reason I don't go near the stuff. The product is too hot, understand. People kill for purified mana. Start wars over it. It wouldn't surprise me if this feud between Laergard and Arethkar came down to nothing but mana crystals. Gosh—now you have me ranting about politics. Seriously, hurry up, I need a drink."

The purple lantern glowed softly in the night. Purified mana, huh? Interesting. The light was reminiscent of the energy ball I had summoned. Though they were different in color. My ball was more of a golden yellow, whereas the lamp light was violet. I hurried behind Shade contemplating everything he had said. I had totally forgotten about the Laergard and Arethkar feud until now. Judging from my most recent quest prompt ("report to the Royal Knights of Laergard") I now knew which continent I was on. I hoped I would have my class sorted out before any giant world changing events happened.

Two guards stood by the entrance to Arondale. They wore bronze metal breast plates and shoulder pads. They had dark green capes and they each held a bayonet-like weapon in their hands. Laergardian soldiers.

The gate between them was no ordinary medieval portcullis but rather a glowing transparent force field. The gate was a thin waterfall of pink energy. The murky contours of a town appeared behind it. It was like staring at a puddle, wincing to make out what lay beneath its surface.

"The gates to the city are closed for the night," said one guard as we approached.

Shade smiled to the guards in reply. "We have urgent business in the city. Perhaps you could open the gate for us."

The guard tilted his head like he was seriously considering it. Shade's luck points and Lirana positive-race bonuses were coming into effect here. But they weren't enough.

"Can't do it," said the guard. "There's been rumors of goblin attacks and the city is on high alert."

"Oh c'mon. There's always rumors of goblin attacks. I'll tell you what, how does a bit of coin affect the gate situation?" Shade pulled out a gold coin and flicked it towards the guard.

The soldier grinned and snatched the coin in the air. He hollered up to the sentry point above us. "Open the gate."

"That was easy enough," I whispered to my companion.

"Says you," said Shade. "You owe me a drink. Make it two."

The gate powered down and the force field flickered and then disappeared completely. As we stepped through the gate, a prompt popped up in my HUD:

You have discovered Arondale! +100 EXP!

Oh sweet. This was to encourage players to travel and explore the world. Another pop-up soon followed.

You've discovered your first waypoint. You can fast travel to any place you've already discovered by opening your world map and selecting the specific waypoint you'd wish to travel to. Price for waypoint depends on how far you're travelling. You can only use waypoints on the continent you're currently in. You can't travel to a waypoint while in combat or in a dungeon.

This would be super handy later on. In-game teleportation was an exciting prospect. For now, though, I closed the prompts and took in a proper sight of Arondale. Crooked wooden buildings leaned over cobblestoned streets. Purple lamp posts lined the walkways. A large blue crystal dome poked out from the red slate roofs near the center of the town. To the east was large cylindrical dome made of glass stained a murky green. All sorts of lights and smoke emanated from the building. Appearing from the other side of it was a giant floating airship with large sails and balloon roof. Radiant pink dust blew out the back of it as it shot forth into the night sky, slowly becoming nothing but a speck in the distance.

"The last airbus to the capital for the night," said Shade, watching the ship disappear into the clouds.

As I followed Shade through the labyrinthine streets, I sensed Arondale was a renaissance town in the midst of a magitech industrial revolution. The streets were smoggy and full of soot. Despite the glowing lampposts, the streets were quiet. We passed pubs and inns full of people drinking and singing. Rorn engineers chugged back pitchers of ale, Muumuu singers performed ballads, Haeren couples danced, and Lirana merchants gambled their earnings away. *The fantasy races in this world had really integrated with each other—or maybe only in more urban dwellings?* I did notice a peculiar lack of Aeri though. A large Rorn knight walked by and knocked his elbow into my chest.

I gasped in pain as my HP bar fell down by 3%. What the hell? My race penalty in action. I really hadn't thought about how shitty these negative alignments were going to be. Stuff like this rarely happened to me back on Earth. This must be what it was like to be a minority in our world. Random penalties becoming obstacles to you just trying to get by.

Shade put his hand on my shoulder. "Maybe keep your head down when passing any Rorn. Especially big ones with massive axes."

The cat rogue continued down the street, his tail wagging behind him. He eventually turned left and we headed through the murky streets in the direction of the airship station. We entered a quiet piazza with a small fountain and through the clearing of the roofs, a windmill stood on a hill beyond the city's western walls. A large red balloon ship laid stationary beside it.

"Who lives over there?"

Shade groaned. "Trust me you don't want to know. Theobold Longstaff. He's the city's local mage. He spends all day surrounded by books because he is beyond boring. Don't worry about him. Hurry."

The wings of the windmill spun gently in the breeze. The magic user lived there, huh? Perfect. I'd go there tomorrow. He'd be the right person to speak to about unlocking my class.

I hurried to catch up with Shade. He had turned into an even smoggier alley than the one we'd just been in. We were in the engineer and blacksmithing district. Shade hurried down another narrow dark alley. No lamps lined the passageway and the only other thing passing through was a scraggly street rat. A normal rat, thankfully.

We went down the alley and Shade stopped in front of a black door with chipped paint and no doorknob. He knocked on the wood.

I grew more and more nervous in the dark alley.

"Where have you brought me?"

"The Crow's Heart. Only the best inn in all of Arondale. If you're one of the lucky few who knows where it is. It operates on purely word of mouth basis."

The door creaked open and we stepped inside a warm candle lit pub. A fireplace crackled in the corner, lighting up the room. A few cloaked figures drank pints by themselves in the back, their hands remained close to the swords sheathed at their sides. The place smelled of smoke, ash, and ale. It was musty enough for me to start coughing which was totally not the badass first impression a place like this demanded from its clientele.

A loud screech came from the bar. I turned to see what the commotion was but didn't see anyone.

"Is that Shade—the scum of the earth who still owes me ten gold coins from getting his butt whooped in a game of cards three nights ago?"

"Uh oh," said Shade. "Relax. I'll handle this."

Two furry ears poked out from behind the bar. The ears hurried passed the wooden table and a middle-aged Muumuu woman appeared. She was under four feet tall and had a bushy orange fox tail that poked through her cotton green dress. She put her hand on her hips and squinted with her big yellow eyes.

"*So*," she said. "What do you have to say for yourself?"

"You were cheating!"

"Better than you were," she scoffed.

I really didn't understand how everyone in Illyria played cards. All I gathered was everyone who played broke the rules on a regular basis.

"Look," said Shade, fluttering his eyelashes flirtatiously at the barmaid. "I had gone out and acquired your ten gold coins but then I got ambushed by a bunch of angry Skren and I only broke out of their encampment a few hours ago. I headed straight here. Honest."

I did recall Shade suggesting we stow ourselves away on an airship to a different continent but now wasn't a good time to mention it.

"A pretty tall tale," sighed the fox woman. "I'm guessing your friend over here can vouch for you."

"Yes he can," said Shade, giving me a painful smack on my back. "Clay meet Eve the owner of this fine establishment. Fair warning: don't let her small stature confuse you, she's the most powerful person in this place. She *sees* and *hears* everything."

The fox woman evaluated me from top to bottom. "Nice to meet you. You look new to these parts. Shame you met this one so quickly. He'll lead you into all sorts of trouble. I assume you'll need room and board?"

I nodded.

"No trouble," she said, heading behind the bar. She grabbed two pint glasses and filled them up at a nearby barrel with an amber ale. "You two sit down and enjoy a pint while I get your rooms ready."

She headed up the stairs of the inn and right as we sat down, she hollered back to Shade: "And don't think for a second your sob story is going to get you off the hook for those coins!"

We took the available table in the middle of the pub. Shade and I clicked our pints together in cheers and each took a long sip. The foamy drink ran down the inside of my neck. It was delicious tasting beer, smooth and flavorsome. The foam was like the platonic ideal of all foam. Within a few sips, my migraine had disappeared and my body had stopped aching. The beer was a potion. It had to be. Only as I drank the ale, filled with its sweet warmth, did it become clear: I had been suffering from hidden dehydration and hunger debuffs. The game would not let you get away with ignoring basic bodily upkeep.

Drinking reminded me of the hostel where I had worked in Paris. Travellers were always nervous and on edge but once you got a beer in their hands, everyone always lightened up. I smiled fondly into my pint glass as I took another sip. Did all food and drinks in Arcane Kingdom Online taste this good?

My ears perked. "Didn't we tell the guards we had urgent business. Aren't we going to go talk to the Royal Knights of Laergard?"

Shade shook his head. "Not now. Our night has been a long one already as it is. We will go to their guild outpost tomorrow. But now we need rest."

He was right. There was nothing to be done at this hour. But I did worry about the mutated Skren lurking somewhere in the forest.

Shade took another long sip of his ale and totally switched gears, telling me a story about the one time he went to bed with a goblin princess the night before her royal wedding. I think Eve was right: Shade was going to bring me loads of trouble. But his story was funny nonetheless. I finished my pint and wished him goodnight.

I headed up the stairs of the inn, the exhaustion of the evening overtaking me. It was time for bed. I found Eve fluffing the pillows in a room and I asked, "May I take this room."

"Certainly," she said. "It's all ready for you."

As she walked past me, she grabbed my wrist and dug her nails into my skin. She stared at me dead in the eye.

"I've left you a pair of gloves on the dresser," she said.

"You don't want to be walking around town in broad daylight with a mark like that on your arm."

"What do you know—"

But she hurried out the door and closed it shut.

I fell onto the bed and considered the swirling dark mark on my right wrist. What the hell did the mutant Skren do to me?

12

###PROGRAM: DREAM TRIGGER##

RUNNING DIAGNOSTICS

....

31454390287987083142093187431

Numbers rushed past me until they fragmented and cracked like smashed glass. I was in a pure white space. In bodiless vapor form like I had been when I first logged in. A silhouette appeared in the distance. The figure moved towards me. The figure got closer. It was a little girl. She had brown hair tied in pig-tails and bright green eyes. She wore red velvet dungarees and she was crying. She ran, screaming, "Help me. Please help me." She reached out her hand

towards me. But I was nothing but air. There was no helping
this girl in my current state.

She clawed at the air, crying and wailing. Next her arm
disintegrated into pixelated cubes. The cubes burst one by
one, destroying her entire arm.

"What's happening to me," she yelled.

The rest of her body did the same, morphing into cubes,
computerized fragments. She screamed as her whole body
disintegrated. The pixilation even crept up her neck, moving
rapidly towards her whole head.

"Please...make it stop...PLEASE!"

I AWOKE IN A SWEAT. I grasped out at the air and pulled at
my yarn blanket. *Where was I?* My fingers were long, thin,
and deathly pale. This wasn't my body. Oh god. What was
happening to me? I rubbed my palms into my eyes. Time to
wake myself from this bizarre dream. Where did the girl go?
Wait—I had been dreaming about her, not this weird
medieval history diorama I've woken up to. Or am I in one
of those dreams within a dream? My HUD flickered in my
retina and it all rushed back to me: the ZERO virus, the
quarantine center, Arcane Kingdom Online, and the cognitive upload. Ugh. Let me go back to bed. Curiosity got the
better of me though. I checked out the window prompts I
had woken to.

> *You have (2) new personal messages*
> *You have (1) new universal message*

I clicked on the prompt and the first message appeared.

Personal Message: Congratulations!

Congratulations Clay Hopewell on successfully surviving your first 24 hours in Arcane Kingdom Online. Our system reports you have a 65% chance of making it through the full integration process. We will update you further later.

Happy adventuring,
TriCorp Dev Team

The words stung full of ominous dread: *We will update you further later.* There was a haunting phrase hanging unsaid. *Or not.* I'll either wake up tomorrow alive or I won't. I'll be dead. It will be goodbye to this new life and world. I shook my head. I didn't want to dwell on it. It was my second day in a new vibrant fantasy world. Wallowing was for suckers.

I closed the TriCorp dev team message and opened the next.

Personal Message: Hello Stranger

Hey Clay! I don't know if you remember me...well I'm sure you do...but it's been a while. It's Serena from college! I'm so happy to see that you're here (or, you know, sad you are here but happy you aren't counting down your life in one of those horrible quarantine centers). Anyways, before I initiated the cognitive upload, I was able to link my Facebook and Gmail friends list to my AKO account so I'd get a notification if anyone I knew joined. You're the first person to enter the game on the same continent as me. Are you able to meet later today? I need to speak to someone. It's very serious and urgent.

Send me your coordinates and I'll use a teleport scroll— hopefully you're somewhere I've already been.

Serena

I leaned my head against the bedframe, taken aback by the pleasant surprise. *Serena Wharton.* She was one of the few friends I had made at college before dropping out. She had worked at the student library where I liked to study and we'd occasionally get coffee after her shift. I smiled as I recalled our conversations. I can't believe she was here. And she wanted to see me. What was so urgent and serious though? Strange. I wrote her back a quick note saying I was in Arondale and when did she want to meet. I moved onto my last message.

Universal Message: Apologies for the Technical Difficulties

A growing number of technical issues have arisen during the launch of A.K.O. this week. If you have experienced anything out of the ordinary, please contact TriCorp dev team. Please bear with us as we sort out these technical issues.

Thank you,
TriCorp Dev Team

I nodded my head at the message, not surprised. Waking up imprisoned in a camp of rat monsters five times your level does sound a lot like a technical problem to me. But I had gotten through it now and there was no use in being bitter. The question was, though, did I report it to TriCorp? The swirling dark mark was still etched in my wrist. For the time being, I'd wait and see if TriCorp fixed the game's issues on their own.

A bell chime went off in my head. Another message had come in. It was Serena again.

Personal Message: Hello Stranger (3)

Arondale will be easy to get to. I have things I need to sort out this morning but how about we meet for 1pm in the church square by the large fountain? See ya then!

I toggled my HUD's interface. It was 8 a.m. game world time. I had five hours to become a mage, get better armor and weapons and not look like a total noob before Serena arrived.

13

I rolled out of the bed, still feeling groggy and strange. My stomach grumbled, demanding breakfast. I headed towards the door and had my hand on the knob when I stopped. The door clicked shut. Eve's voice echoed through my head: *You don't want to be walking around town in broad daylight with a mark like that on your arm.* The swirling dark whirlpool stared up at me, drawing me closer into its gaze. I pulled away and went over to the dresser. I found a pair of green leather gloves sitting on top.

> *New Item Alert! Leather Gloves of the Mind (TGH: 3. MP+5. Durability 9/10)*
> *Do you wish to equip (Yes/No)?*

Yes please. The gloves flickered out of my hands and within seconds my fingers were covered. I didn't even think to put them on manually; the near instant materializing was too cool to pass up. These gloves were awesome. The +5 MP bonus was a sweet bonus stat. It meant one more energy blast in battle before I ran out of mana. I'd have to thank Eve for these. They also did the trick of covering my wrists which was their intended purpose. I would have to investigate this mark eventually. Right now though, let's make it through the morning.

I found Shade downstairs, sitting at a stool at the bar, with a half-full pint in his hand. His tail was wagging as he bantered with Eve.

"Isn't it a little early for beer?"

"In my book, there's no better way to start the day," said Shade, taking a long sip. He licked off a lingering foam moustache with his tongue. "Of course, I don't have an actual book. It's an expression. A figure of speech." He burped. How many of those pints had he already slung back this morning?

"Don't mind him," said Eve, polishing the bar with a rag. "Sit down and have breakfast. It's not every day I have an Aeri passing through here. People say an Aeri's presence brings good luck. In my case, more customers."

I walked over to the stool and sat down beside Shade. He nudged me with his elbow. "Pint?"

"I'm okay," I said.

"Suit yourself." The Lirana shrugged and took another slurp of his beer.

I turned to Eve who brought me over a basket of bread slices. Inside the basket was a knife and two small jars, one with butter and another with blueberry jam. "Thanks Eve," I said as I picked up a piece of bread. With the knife I spread a layer of butter over the bread slice followed by a layer of jam. I took a bite of the bread and instantly felt a wave of joy pass through me. The butter was incredibly smooth and blended with the intensely flavorful jam perfectly. The bread was fresh and had this wonderful fluffy texture. I chowed down the bread in a couple of bites and dressed up a new slice right after. Soon the slices were a mere pile of crumbs and even those were yummy enough to pick at with my fingers. When I finished, a prompt came up on my HUD:

Well-Fed (Buff): There's nothing better than a good meal.
+2 to all stats (Duration: 30 minutes)

This game was definitely going to turn me into a fat ass with these kinds of bonuses. My HUD faded and Shade placed his pint down emphatically and stretched his arms. "Well let's not burn any more daylight—shall we head off?"

I got off my stool and Shade tipped his head to Eve. I waved and said, "Thanks again for the bread and the gloves."

Eve waved my thanks aside.

"Keep that one out of trouble and don't take those gloves off, you hear."

I nodded and followed Shade out the door.

Arondale was a totally different place in the morning than it had been at night. Noise abounded: the hollers of builders and workmen, the banging hammers of black-smiths, the rush of feet and garbled conversation in a variety of exotic languages. Airships swooshed above us, blocking out the sun and draping us briefly in their shadows, as they flew across the sky towards the major cities of Laergard. Arondale was a town situated halfway between the major cities of the Eastern Laergardian continent. It was a hub for nearby farmers and artisans to sell their raw materials to craftsmen and merchants who would then sell the unique items further afield. It blew my mind to think this was one of the smaller urban dwellings in Laergard.

We stepped out of the Crow's Heart alley and into a busy thoroughfare. What had been an empty cobble-stoned street the night before was now a bustling road full of market stalls. Under different colored canopies were dealers selling rare and powerful jewels, magic scrolls, high level armor and weaponry and everything in between. It was all far out of my price range so I fought the urge to ogle over the cool wares. The thing I found most distracting were the food stalls. There were farmers selling fresh produce: thick delicious carrots, bright green lettuce leaves, onions, turnips. One stall was serving mugs of apple cider, spiced with sugar and cinnamon. All the crates full of fruit made my mouth water. Everything I'd already tasted in A.K.O. had been delicious; my hungry eyes told me the market food would be even more so.

I shook my head at the thought. No. I needed to sell the loot I'd gained from last night and get new armor and a better weapon if it had an affordable price tag. I'd treat myself to cider and pie once I was a successful adventurer.

I turned my head away from the stalls just in time to dodge a man rushing passed us, pushing a wheelbarrow full of boxed crates. He hurried ahead towards the aerodome with his delivery.

We continued through the market stalls, ambling along, enjoying the gorgeous morning: a bright blue sky hung above with white clouds drifting aimlessly in the air. The day had a Spring quality, with the warm sun and the gentle breeze. I was optimistic, excited for the potentials A.K.O. had to offer.

"Shade," I said, grabbing him by the shoulder as he pushed his way through the crowd of merchants and passing travellers. "Before we go to the guild hall—is there a merchant you'd recommend where I can sell my loot and pick up decent armor?"

Shade's eyebrows jumped with excitement. "I know just

the guy and we have time to kill. Guild Hall doesn't open until around nine anyway."

We hurried past a few more stalls and stopped in front of a building with a thatched roof and mullioned windows. Beside the wooden door was a sign engraved with drawing of a sword, shield, and a pile of coins. A one-stop shop. A classic general store.

The door barely opened. Through a tiny sliver we managed to squeeze through. The inside was cluttered with junk, from dusty armor to old books with torn away pages. I struggled to breathe in the musty shop.

"Oi! Frederick—you here?" said Shade walking delicately through the shop, making sure not to knock anything over.

Popping out from an indiscriminate pile of rags was a middle-aged Haeren man, sporting a thick brown moustache. He raised his hands in the air and said, "Welcome to my shop, humble travellers. Please browse my wares and let me know if you need any assistance."

I smiled at the man and perused the shop. I stopped in front of a two-handed great sword. I reached out to pick it up, yet when I gripped the handle I didn't have the strength to lift it out of its place. Was it enchanted or something? I scanned the item:

Old Iron Great Sword* (ATKP: 50-60. Durability 8/10)
*Only usable by classes with skills in two-handed
weaponry such as Warrior or Blade Knight

The sword was really cool. It made me question my goal to become a spellcaster. But then I noticed an epic staff hanging on a shelf in the back and I instantly forgot about the sword. The staff was made of ancient wood and the top of it held a jagged crystal.

"How much is that?"

Frederick the shopkeeper laughed. "Definitely out of your price range is what it is."

Clearly my status as a new player was obvious. I wore goofy bandit gear not fit for an Aeri. It was barely a cut above the gear everyone started with before they branched into more class appropriate gear.

"Do you have any gear more suitable for someone like me?"

Frederick looked me up and down and rubbed his chin. "You don't have an identifiable class so your options are limited. But judging from your race and build, I imagine you'll want something on the more lighter side; something good for a magic user, perhaps?"

I nodded my head. "Sounds great. Do you have anything?"

He peered around the cluttered mess he called a shop floor. How anyone knew where something was in here was beyond me. But clearly there was a method to Frederick's madness as he suddenly had an "aha" moment and rushed over to one corner and dug out a dark green coat with matching pants.

Green Apprentice Coat (DEF: 11. Durability 9/10)
Green Apprentice Pants (DEF: 9. Durability 9/10)

My eyes widened at the apparel. Along with my gloves and boots this would push my bonus Defense to +25, which would be amazing and go a long way to increasing my survivability. Plus the aesthetic suited my Aeri build. It was elegant and had a velvety softness and sheen to it. It was the apparel of a kickass wizard. Or, you know, one in training.

"I'll give you a deal on both. How does 100 gold coins sound?"

My jaw dropped. My bank account currently stood at 0 coins. It was time to barter my items before I got attached to any other gear.

"Do you buy gear as well?"

"Of course," said Frederick. "What do you got for me?"

I opened my inventory tab and unloaded the full set of rough leather Skren gear I'd taken off one of the bandits yesterday.

"How much for all of this?"

"Hmm," said Frederick. "It's all a bit rough. But it's a decent full set. How does 25 gold coins for the armor and 10 for the sword sound?"

35 gold wasn't nearly as much as I had been hoping for. The rough leather gear I currently wore would net me a further 25 which would get me up to 60 gold pieces. Still not enough though. What about the Skren tails!

"How much are these worth?"

Frederick's eyes widened at them. I don't think he was expecting such loot off a beginner like me. "I can give 20 gold coins for the three tails."

That would bring me up to 80 gold coins which still wasn't enough.

Time to try a new tactic. I blinked my eyes and frowned at Frederick.

"Would you sell the set to me for 80?"

Frederick chuckled and shook his head. "Nope. You already made it clear to me how desperately you want them. You'll get me the 100 somehow I'm sure of it."

Barter (Level 1) Failed
You increased your bartering skills by 0.1

I examined the prompt further and a new page appeared.

Bartering (Passive Skill)
Bartering is one of the primary skills of merchants and craftsmen but can be utilized by all classes for a variety of benefits. Improve your bartering skills by negotiating with others and persuading them to see things your way. Remember: the best deals are when both parties walk away feeling as if they won.

This was good to know for the future. I accidentally played my hand with Frederick but I wouldn't let it happen again so easily. It did give me another idea though. A.K.O. had a pretty basic JRPG stat system for character leveling. The real meat and complexity of the game came in the form of all the other different skills and abilities you learned and leveled outside of your base stats. The bartering prompt was making me consider all the other crafting abilities available to unlock.

I asked Frederick to excuse me for one second as I headed over to Shade to ask him a question. The cat man was currently holding up a cotton ball of thread and holding it above his head, mesmerized. When I spoke to him, he snapped out of the trance.

"Shade—why are the Skren rat tails so valuable again?"

"They're an uncommon delicacy and can be used in cooking to make a variety of different things. I had a Skren sandwich once with mustard and Solmini cheese," Shade said wistfully.

I had an idea.

I headed back over to Frederick and took him up on his offer to take the Skren bandit gear and sword for 35 gold coins. I then told him I'd come back to him later with the gold needed for the apprentice apparel.

As I rushed out the door, Shade followed behind saying, "I don't like that crazed look in your eye mate. What are you up to?"

I walked over to one of the produce stalls and asked for the price of a bushel of onions. The Lirana farm lady said, "7 gold coins?"

"How about five," I asked.

She shook her head.

Barter (Level 1) Failed
You increased your bartering skills by 0.1

I glanced around to the other produce stalls, letting the merchant know I had plenty of options. The farm lady saw this and said, "Five gold coins it is."

Barter (Level 1) Success
You increased your bartering skills by 0.3

She handed me the bushel of onions. I turned around and handed them to Shade. "Hold these, please."

Next I hurried over to a spice merchant—a dark eyed man with sandy blonde hair. He struck me as Haeren but not Laergardian. He had the air of a very conniving merchant. The man had a whole table of wooden boxes with alluring different herbs, leaves, and spices. All perfect for cooking. But I was only after one thing. The simplest ingredient of all.

"I'd like a small bag of salt please?"

The spice merchant's mouth opened in a yellow gap-toothed grin. He leaned over and picked up a small bag of salt.

"10 gold coins."

Highway robbery. I'm sure for someone a couple of levels higher the ten coins would hardly matter, but I was penny pinching.

"How about 7?"

The man shook his head. "Go somewhere else. I don't care."

Barter (Level 1) Failed
You increased your bartering skills by 0.1

He wasn't going to budge but it was worth a try. Even if I failed, my barter skill went up.

This plan better work, I thought as I handed him the ten coins.

I needed one last thing, but I wasn't sure it would exist in Illyria. I turned to Shade, who was begrudgingly following me around with the bushel of onions, and said, "Do you know what a stock cube is?"

His eyes narrowed quizzically and he shook his head. "There you go being all strange again, talking about made up things like 'stock cubes.'"

"It's this thing where I'm from. It's a burst of flavor. It replicates chicken or beef stock."

"Oh like stock jelly. Eve has loads of those in her kitchen."

Perfect.

I turned back around and headed through the crowds until we were back at the Crow's Heart. I knocked on the door confidently and it swung wide open. I stepped inside and found Eve behind the bar.

"Eve—I need your help. Do you mind if I borrow your kitchen?"

"For you, anything. So long as he stays outside," she glared at Shade.

The Lirana handed me the bushel of onions and shrugged as he stepped back outside. I headed into a small cove area which made up Eve's kitchen. There was a fireplace stovetop with a cauldron. Rummaging through her kitchen utensils, I found a sharp chopping knife; this would do the trick. It was time to get to work.

I asked Eve to light the stove and boil water for me as I chopped the onions. I sliced and diced the onions quite quickly. Like eerily faster than I normally would. When I finished cutting up the onions, I scraped them off the chop board into the hot cauldron. They sizzled and a rich smell rose from the pot. Nothing like cooking with fresh ingredients.

As I did this the same prompt kept popping in my HUD.

You increased your cooking skills by 0.1
You increased your cooking skills by 0.1
You increased your cooking skills by 0.1

I materialized the large Skren tails from my inventory and placed them on the cutting board. I wiped my eye, sighed and got to work. The knife sliced through the rat tail with ease. I chopped the tails up into cubes and then threw them in with the onions.

Meanwhile Eve was boiling a kettle of hot water for me which I then poured into the pot. Next I grabbed the stock jelly from the counter and threw it in. A bright light glowed out from the cauldron and a prompt appeared across my HUD:

> *You have discovered a new recipe: Simple Skren*
> *Tail Stew*
> *Ingredients: Onion, Skren Tail, Salt, Chicken Stock Jelly*
> *A bowl of Simple Skren Tail Stew offers you +30%*
> *damage against all Skren*
> *(Duration: 30 minutes)*

> *Your cooking skills increased by 0.7*
> *You've leveled up Cooking (craft) to Level 2*

The stew smelt fantastic and I had purchased the ingredients and made it all in under half an hour. The recipe was based off an old chicken stew one I used to make at the hostel when our cook was sick. It was an old simple classic but it appealed to the hungover travellers passing through our doors. I was happy to see the stew still worked with the new Skren tail ingredient.

A finger tapped the side of my ribs. I turned around and saw Eve standing behind me.

"Are you planning on eating it all?" she asked, "Because there's a line up outside."

Hungry warriors and merchants had lined up outside, drawn to the Crow's Heart by the smell of my stew. This was going even better than I expected.

Eve and I cut a deal. She'd provide the serving bowls and we'd sell each bowl for ten gold apiece. We had about twenty bowls worth in the pot. Since we had used Eve's cooking utensils she wanted a cut of the profits. I said if we sold it all I'd give her 40% of our cut.

We sold out in minutes. We split the gold out, Eve taking

80 coins and me pocketing the rest. I greedily eyed my inventory screen as the gold coin symbol shot up to 140. Unbelievable. The game was offering me a potential whole other path of life. I didn't have to necessarily go around killing monsters and going on quests. The life of a craftsmen —a restaurateur!—was within my grasp.

I thanked Eve again and hurried out back through the market and over to Frederick's. The apprentice coat and pants were still there.

"Are you still interested in the offer?" asked the portly merchant picking at his moustache."

Do you wish to purchase:

Green Apprentice Coat (TGH: 11. Durability 9/10)
Green Apprentice Pants (TGH: 9. Durability 9/10)

For the price of: 100 gold coins

Yes/No ?

I said yes. The number of gold coins in my inventory dropped to 40 and two new items appeared within my five available slots. I instantly selected them to be equipped.

Instantaneously, my beginner leather gear was off and I was clad in a long dark green jacket falling just below my knees. The wool jacket came with a slinky hood which I would keep down as to not look suspicious. Puffy trousers in a matching color hung below my waist over my rough leather boots. The dusty mirror revealed someone who had a firm grasp of magic and the ability to summon fire with a flick of their fingers. One day maybe.

With my new gear on, I sold the old leather junk for

another 25 gold. I didn't want it taking up space in my inventory. Which reminded me of something.

"Do you have anything to increase inventory space Frederick?"

"Yes," said the shopkeeper. "Give me one moment."

He rummaged around and brought over a simple brown leather backpack. "This is an apprentice backpack. Gives you fifteen additional slots of inventory space. I can sell it to you for 65 gold?"

All my money, huh? The extra inventory space sounded nice. Less item management.

"How about for 40 gold," I said. "You know because I've bought so much from you already."

It was a low-ball bid but I hoped he'd meet me halfway. Instead, he nodded and said, "Works for me."

Barter (Level 1) Success!
You increased your bartering skills by 0.4
You've leveled up Bartering (Passive Skill) to Level 2

I walked out of the shop with my new backpack and gear.

"Well don't you look good," said Shade, leaning against the wall outside of Frederick's shop. "Ready to visit the Royal Knights of Laergard?"

"Hell yeah," I said, gripping the handles of my recently acquired backpack as I strutted down the road, showing off my new and slightly less noobish look.

14

The market stalls dwindled as we headed west across the city. We passed other squares with small churches and fountains, went through quiet neighborhood streets where Lirana and Muumuu women were hanging out laundry to dry from their windowsills. We crossed a bridge over a bright green canal and entered a piazza. In a few steps the city had completely changed: gone were the narrow laneways, the graffiti, the cracked and dirty cobblestoned streets. No beggars laid on the ground here, hats out asking for coins. Nope—the streets here were clean, bright in their magnificence, lush green trees poking their pretty branches into the street beyond the courtyard walls from which they came.

A few Haeren men and woman strolled across the square in bright Victorian garments. The woman wore puffy dresses with crinoline cages underneath and the men strutted about in suits and waistcoats with gilded buttons. They were walking along a shopping street with brightly lit windows, browsing clothing and other luxury items. There was an instrument shop selling lutes and fiddles and other goods important to anyone in the bard class. The window of a fancy butcher caught my eye: a large carcass of a magnificent boar hung from the window, above jars of special horseradish and other artisanal spices.

Shade groaned. "Ugh—this is why I hate coming to *west* Arondale. I have to acknowledge such people exist."

"Who are they?"

"Nobles of the city," Shade explained. "Sons and daughters of very wealthy merchants or cousins of the Royal family. Doesn't matter which. Let's ignore them and head on our way."

We kept moving through the pretty streets of Arondale's wealthy neighborhood, passing large homes and columned gates. The streets weren't as packed as the east end of the city but there were still plenty of people passing us by: from well-dressed nobles to fully armored knights. I eyed everyone who hurried by—mages, paladins, rangers, and an assortment of classes and races in different combinations—and it was impossible to tell the difference between any of them and Shade. There was nothing outwardly distinguishable about the players and NPCs. Besides we were all bits of code now anyway. But some sets of code—the players—came back to life after being killed. Death was all the more real to NPCs. Would they come to resent the so-called Chosen?

At the end of the road, we approached a large building made of a light red stone. On either side of the archway entrance hung two green banners. The banners featured a large symbol of a shield, stitched seamlessly in silver thread across the green background. The herald of the Royal Knights of Laergard. A shield. I liked how it privileged defense and justice over strength and power. A banner with clashing swords would've put me ill at ease. I hoped the iconography matched the personalities of this guild.

We approached the archway where two guards, similar to the ones outside the city, raised their hands to halt us.

"Who visits the guildhall of the Royal Knights of Laergard?"

I was about to open my mouth and launch into the whole story about being kidnapped by Skren and attacked by a demon monster when Shade bowed his head and waved his arm in this elegant and totally out-of-character manner.

"Excuse us," said Shade, keeping his head down in a diminutive posture. "But we ran into trouble last night in the woods and would greatly like to pass on the message of a foul creature lurking in the woods to your captain. Do you mind if we step through to your courtyard?"

The guards nodded, giving us their approval. They stepped out of our way.

"You're lucky. Captain Edward Silver is in the back training the new recruits," said one of the guards. "Speak to him."

We walked passed the guards and Shade did not acknowledge his complete change in diction and personality beyond a subtle smirk on his face. The Lirana luck bonuses and positive racial alignments clearly knew no bounds.

Loud clangs of clashing swords and grunts echoed through the shadowy tunnel leading to the guild's courtyard. Stepping into the quad, a large training ground was revealed to us. Rows of armored soldiers practiced stabbing with their bayonets, others were working on their shield stances, a few fought with swords off to the side. Most of the soldiers were Haeren, but there were a couple of bulky Rorn soldiers in the training crowd.

In one corner, two soldiers caught my attention. One of them was sweaty and red in the face. He was overheating in his armor. The other dragged his sword on the ground, unable to lift it up.

"Why can't I wield this damn thing?"

"You need to put more attribute points into Attack Power and Toughness," whispered the other one.

So they were players. They must be working on a quest to unlock the warrior or knight class. Interesting. Part of me wanted to go over and talk to them. It would be comforting to talk with someone else from back home. But I wasn't sure. These were the kinds of decisions you made all the time as a backpacker, split second judgment calls on people. People new to backpacking would always say hello to other travellers—becoming instant friends. But the longer you stayed on the road, the more cautious you were, the more you sussed out an individual, making sure they weren't a crazy person you'd be attaching yourself to for the next couples of hours, days, or even weeks. I grinned as Shade's sensitive whiskers caused his face to dart all around the courtyard. I was already caught up with one weirdo. No need for any more.

In the center of the courtyard was one particular knight, barking orders at the others. He wore a suit of silver armor with no helmet: it was beautifully polished, sun bouncing off the smoothness, giving him a light glow. He had long black hair tucked behind his ears and the faded remains of a scar over his left eye. Soldiers came up to him with scrolls and he quickly signed them.

Captain Edward Silver.

Shade and I walked towards him.

All the guards in the courtyard spun on their boots. The wind swooshed in our direction. Every blade and rifle in the vicinity was pointed directly at our necks.

"Whoah," I said.

The knight we'd been approaching, lifted his hand with a closed fist. He'd make the decision as to whether or not we'd be harmed.

"Speak trespassers. What do you wish with the Royal Knights of Laergard?"

I gulped and waited for Shade to say something. He didn't. The blades at our throat made him nervous and hindered his charisma.

"We come to pass on information," I said, my voice cracking. "We believe there is a powerful monster lurking in the woods. It threatens the greater good of Arondale and the surrounding area."

The grizzled knight looked me straight in the face. His stare sought to separate me from my words, finding the truth somewhere between them. His wearied faded eyes glinted with the sad recognition of someone who has witnessed their own share of unspeakable horrors.

Shade nudged me and whispered in my ear. "Mention the reward."

Edward Silver lowered his hands and the soldiers did the same with their weapons.

"Everyone, back to your drills," shouted the knight. "You two, come with me."

The knight turned his back to us and walked towards the western edge of the courtyard where he entered a stone arcade. He led us to a burgundy door. He opened it and gestured with his gauntleted hand for us to enter.

The room was dark but for a window in the corner letting in a ray of natural light and a small mana lamp on the oak desk, tingeing the room with its soft purple glow. Behind the desk was a large map with five floating continents. Illyria. It was an awe-inspiring image. I'd seen a tiny speck of what this world had to offer. Every moment—but especially this one—reminded me of the amazing feat TriCorp had achieved in creating this game. They really had created another world. The knight closed the door and moved passed us to his desk. He turned away from us, watching his practicing soldiers from the window.

"Explain to me from the beginning what happened."

I retold the whole story, leaving out the part where I had died and come back. I wasn't sure how safe it was to tell people I was one of the Chosen.

"The creature, you say, came back to life, reincarnated with the soul of a demon?"

I shrugged. "Yeah."

The knight shook his head. He spoke softly, "The Royal Knights of Laergard are sworn to protect the realm. But the current tensions simmering between ourselves and Arethkar have the Royal family paranoid and suspicious. All of our men are training and preparing for an attack on Land's Shield or Claren's Crossing. We don't have the resources to be protecting the interior as we have in the past." He turned from the window. "The problem you speak of, though, deeply concerns me. If we can't defend our own land from the inside, how will we ever protect it from those coming from beyond? Give me time to gather a small group to scour the nearby woods for later this afternoon. Your continued assistance in this matter would be greatly appreciated."

A prompt appeared in my HUD.

Quest Update: Mysterious Creature in the Wood

*Join Captain Edward Silver and the Royal Knights of
Laergard in a hunting expedition of S^%AD"@@@@@
later this afternoon.*

*Quest Type: Unique
Quest Difficulty: Hard
Reward: 100 EXP + ?*

I shivered as I read over the update. I noticed the quest
difficulty had now changed from moderate to hard. More
frightening was the fact the game engine still hasn't been
able to define the mutated Skren bandit leader. The game
was propelling us towards fighting this glitch. Or was the
virus orchestrating our own downfall? We'd have to go face
this thing to learn more about it and—the dark mark underneath my gloves ached—whatever it had done to me.

I nodded my head to Captain Edward Silver. "We'll
gladly join you on your expedition. We'll return here later
this afternoon."

The knight crossed his arms and grunted approvingly.
He was impressed.

I hoped by the afternoon he would have actual reason
to be.

15

When we passed through the entrance and returned to the
street, Shade turned his head back and forth suspiciously.

"Is everything okay?"

He blinked and said, "Listen—I have errands I need to
run, people I need to speak to, coins I need to gamble,
drinks I need drink, you know the drill—so I'll leave you on
your own for the next little while, okay? I'd invite you along
but you don't strike me as someone eager for the thieving
life. So I'll see you later alright." He threw his furry hand out
to be shaken and I grabbed it with mine. "Good call not
asking for a reward, it will definitely show up at the end of
this whole thing. Or at least I hope so."

The thief spun around and ran off down the street, his
tail wagging behind him.

I took a long sigh. I was on my own again. Shade's
company would be missed. But I'll see him later this
afternoon.

I checked the time on my HUD. It was only 9:30 a.m. I
still had hours before my meeting with Serena and even
longer till my quest with Captain Edward Silver. Above the

walls of the city, cutting across the bright blue sky was the large windmill tower and the bright airship with the red balloon. The home of Theobold Longstaff. It was calling out to me, beckoning me towards it. I had to get my class unlocked and the place to do it was right there.

I headed down the road. I was already close to the walls of the city. It was a matter of finding an exit point. At the end of the street, I found two guards standing by an open gate. No mana shield until sun down. Standing near the guard was a woman with a straw hat on. She had a wheelbarrow full of glass bottles. Half were filled with red liquid while the rest had blue colored water.

"Off to go adventuring," asked the woman. "Fancy a potion?"

Crap, potions! They were my top priority to buy yesterday and I ended up spending all my money on new gear.

"How much are they?"

"I got small health potions and small mana potions. Both cost 10 gold coins each."

I scanned the red potion bottle to get more information.

Small Health Potion (Restores 50 HP)

I placed the bottle down and picked up the mana potion.

Small Mana Potion (Restores 50 MP)

I went with one of each. One would save me from being killed and one would help me kill something faster. Both were important to have. I bartered with the merchant but she wouldn't budge and eventually I relented to her price. Each potion appeared in a slot in my inventory page while

20 gold coins disappeared, leaving me with only 5 gold for the time being.

I thanked the merchant and turned towards the open gate. I nodded my head at the guards and passed through the opening in the wall, discovering a gorgeous meadow outside. The grass was bright green and full of yellow flowers. Bumblebees the size of my fist floated about, landing on flower petals. Similar sized-mosquitoes buzzed in the air, not moving much, hovering in the open field. A couple of rabbits hopped over the tall grass. Wind gently brushed everything to the side. In the distance, a few players hacked away with their rusty swords at the bumblebees. The monsters' red bar of hit points lowered beneath their captions. I smiled. Finally. A beginner zone.

I pulled out my rusty sword and stretched the fingers of my energy ball hand. The windmill was just up the hill but the temptation of low level grinding was too much to resist. I approached the nearest bumblebee.

Bumblebee
Level 1

All the information I got. No HP or MP stats because I no longer had Shade, with his analyze ability, in my party. The bee was freaky; I'd never seen one so big. It's smooth jet black eyeballs stared out at me, waiting for me to make the first move. It hovered there with its six spindly legs, hanging from its furry black and yellow body. I had distance on it, so I would shoot it from range first. I gathered the energy inside me and let it course through to the palm of my hand. I angled my arm so my palm was pointing right at the bee like a rifle. Next I let my fingers stretch out, releasing the energy ball and letting it fly at the bee. The blast knocked it right in the eyes, draining its health bar of a third of its HP.

The bee fluttered manically in the air. It regained its balance and shot towards me. Uh oh. I summoned another energy ball but it flew at me faster than I expected and I lost my concentration. It spun right up to my face, its antennae poking against my face, its long clear tongue hanging out of its mouth. Ick! I swiped the air with my sword. But the bee buzzed around me avoiding my hits. I had to get away from it and attack it at a distance again.

But when I moved away, my feet wobbled and I didn't go in the direction I wanted. Meanwhile the bee was still zooming in and out of my face. I swatted at it with my sword to no avail. My sword wasn't even close to hitting the bee; every time I swung downward, my arm would go to the side or do the opposite. My body wasn't listening to me.

Confusion (Debuff): You have been confused. Up is down, right is left—what is even happening? Movement speed -5%, muddled motions (duration: 30 seconds)

So I was helpless for thirty seconds, basically. I tried to get the hang of maneuvering my body differently but it was too difficult. Next the bee dug its stinger into my forehead, creating a burst of pain in my head. Through tears of frustration, my HUD let me know the attack only did about 3 HP. Pittance. But if the bee kept me confused, it had a good chance of slowly killing me. I had to get away from it.

I waddled backwards and forwards like a madman until eventually I willed myself to step forward—and relief and sanity returning to me—I did so. Instantly I ran from the bee, hoping to gain space between us. I turned towards the bee—now a few meters behind. I powered up an energy ball and let out a blast taking out another third of its HP. The blast also screwed up the insect's momentum. It floated in its own confused stasis as I charged up another energy ball and finished the monster off.

+35 EXP!

I approached the dead shell of the bee as I breathed heavily in and out. You had to be careful with every creature in this world; they all had a strategy or pattern of attack they would kill you with. I scanned the dead bee for loot:

New Item(s) Alert!
Bee Needle (x1)
Jar of Honey (x1)

I ripped the stinger off the bug to add it to my inventory. The other loot item confused me. I didn't see a jar of honey anywhere. How was it possible a bumblebee carried around a glass jar of honey anyways? I crouched down and lifted my sword to its hard insect stomach and drew a long incision through it. I split the bee carcass into two and—closing my eyes—slipped my hand into its slimy and chitinous insides. My fingers wrapped around something cold. I pulled my hand out of the bee carcass and discovered a small glass jar of beautiful honey in my palm. It dematerialized as I added it to my inventory. I grinned as I stood up off the ground. I was happy with the loot, laughing to myself at the sheer craziness of living in a world dictated by video game logic.

I stood up, wiped the dirt off my pants, and noticed while I had dissected the dead bumblebee my HP and MP had fully restored to maximum. They must regenerate faster when not in battle. This was useful information. Something to be exploited here in this beginner zone. I grinned as I eyed another nearby bee and powered up an energy ball. I stretched out my arm and intuitively it locked into the perfect position to shoot. It was like an in-game auto-accuracy. It wasn't perfect but it nudged you in the right direction. I'd noticed it when fighting the Skren bandits. How else had I been able to swing a sword properly?

I stayed a good distance from the bee. I launched the blast and hit the bee, stunning it into confusion. I powered up another blast. It snapped out of its muddled state and rushed me. I unleashed the energy ball.

+35 EXP

The kill was less satisfying than the last one. I knew how to kill these things now. They were super susceptible to magic attacks and if you hit them from range, they had zero chance of hurting you because they would die before even getting close. I rushed over to its body and picked up the bee needle and—cutting it open and reaching inside—the jar of honey as well.

I would try something different next. Off in the distance was a mosquito, floating in the air. It stretched out to a larger size than the bumblebee, but its thin scraggly legs made it less intimidating. The clear wings flapped so rapidly they were a buzzing blur behind the insect. I would try the same strategy I used on the bee. I waited for my MP to fully restore and then charged up an energy ball and shot it at him. I briefly hoped for a one-shot instakill but I was sorely disappointed.

Missed!

Are you kidding me? The mosquito didn't even attack me. It moved around and then fell back into it waiting position again. Fluke. I manipulated the mana inside of me, forming a ball in my palm again and shot the ball of energy at the mosquito. I closed my eyes, waiting for the rush of experience points. I opened them only to see the same annoying prompt on my HUD as last time.

Missed!

I gripped my sword. It was time to change strategy. I headed towards the mosquito slowly. I took one soft step, then another. When I got close enough to stare at the mosquitos beady eyes and squiggly legs I lifted my sword high in the air and swung down, crashing into the mosquito's skull. I knocked off a quarter of its HP. I swung down again but the mosquito had now ducked beyond my sword's hit box.

Despite the melee attack's success, I didn't want to stay in the vicinity of the mobile bug in fear of it confusing me like the bee so I jumped and ran backwards. The bug zipped and glided through the air towards me. I charged up an energy ball. It hadn't worked earlier but the bug was no longer in its zen like state and was now after my blood. Enraged it wouldn't be able to dodge as effectively. I shot the energy ball at the bug and the hit landed, stunning it into immobility. I ran towards it and swung my sword, dealing the final death blow.

+35 EXP!

The mosquito's crinkled body fell to the ground and I scanned it for loot.

New Item Alert! Mosquito Wing (x2)
Do you wish to add to your inventory (Yes/No)?

I didn't know what use the mosquito wings were, but I'd thought the same way about the Skren rat tails and they were what paid for all my new gear. I bent over and pulled the clear and delicate wings off the mosquito's shriveled corpse.

A rabbit hopped through the grass nearby. My next target. The potential loot drops made my mouth water. Rabbit meat stew. Rabbit fur gloves. The bunny was a treasure trove of crafting materials. I took one step towards it and it darted into a large patch of grass and disappeared. Damn it.

Over the course of my grinding, the field had changed. The bumblebee mobs were no longer floating about by themselves. They were now roaming together in packs of two or three. They recognized the danger I posed and so the respawned bees had smarted up to my behavior. Interesting. So the creatures or the algorithms behind them weren't simply mindless patterns on repetition. There was serious A.I. working behind the scenes of these bumblebee mobs. This was an important piece of information I'd have to keep in the back of my head. The fact the mobs changed their behavior and pattern of attack meant it would be immensely difficult to exploit their movement as they continuously changed and adapted to their environment. This was life or death information.

So screw you bees. I wasn't going to fall for your trap. I slid my sword back into its sheath and headed towards the windmill house at the top of the hill. It was time to unlock my class.

16

I walked away from the beginner leveling zone and up the hill of the meadow. As I approached the top of the hill, I passed through a small dirt road, lined with apple trees. The red apples glowed out to me and the thought of more crafting materials made me swerve in their direction. My mind raced with all the potential recipes available with apples in my inventory. But what if these apples were grown by the mysterious Theobold? Would he reprimand me for stealing his fruit? Chill. I was overthinking it. Under the shade of the gnarled fruit tree, I reached up to a branch and pulled off an apple.

New Item Alert! Apple (x1)
Do you wish to add to your inventory (Yes/No)?

The apple disappeared out of the palm of my hand and into my backpack. There were still a dozen more apples hanging in the tree. What was the harm in taking a few more?

I grabbed the tree with both hands and gave it a good shake. A few more apples fell from the tree, one even knocked me on the head. As I bent over to pick the first one up, something else fell onto my head. It didn't have the hard thump of the apple. It had landed gently. Legs ruffled through my hair. Uh oh—what the hell was on me? I dropped the apple in my hand and waved my hands through my hair, knocking away the bug on my head.

I turned around, unsheathing my sword, ready to face whatever had attacked me. Crawling at my feet was a spider as big as a football. It had grey fuzzy hair and thick legs. It must have been napping in the shade of the apple tree when I disturbed it. I took in its caption and full red health bar.

Spider
Level 1

Let's get this over with. I charged up an energy ball and knocked it back, taking off a fifth of its HP. I ran up to it and swung my sword like I was wielding a hammer and did another couple of damage, dealing blows to its abdomen. I charged up another energy ball and blasted it at the spider close range. The arachnid shot back across the road, digging its claws into the ground to slow the momentum of the blast.

The close-range attack had done quite a bit of extra damage. I'll try and remember this against other arachnid enemies. The spider spun around and hurried away. Oh hell no. It didn't attack me and start running when the battle went bad. Those experience points were mine. I fired up an energy ball and swung it at the creature. It crumpled to the floor.

+35 EXP!

I ran over to its dead body and looted its remains, gaining eight spider legs. I went back to the apple tree—and without shaking it this time—picked up the apples already on the ground.

I wiped the dirt off my pants. Through the branches of the apple trees loomed the windmill in the distance. The wings spun in a gentle circle, providing, power and energy to the attached home. The windmill was actually one of three sections, connected by brick hallways. There was an octagonal building with a thatched roof which must have been the mage's living quarters. Attached to it was a small tower with a domed glass roof, with the lens of a telescope built into it. Thin metal pipes crawled up the building like vines.

Despite its shabbiness—crooked pipes and worn walls —the building had a wondrous and majestic quality. The dirt path through the apple orchard led directly to the front door. It was painted red and had a carving of two half-moons and a star. I took a deep breath, raised my back straight, and knocked on the door.

Silence.

I knocked again and this time someone yelled: "Go away. I'm at work."

This was a test, I kept telling myself. A test to see how determined I was to unlock the mage class. I knocked again.

A loud clang and clamor echoed from inside the home. There was the noisy blast of a small explosion. Angry foot-steps got louder and louder until the door swung open, revealing a stocky old Rorn, the veins on his forehead pulsating with irritation. The man had grey hair tied back in a tight pony-tail and a braided beard. He wore an impressive red velvet coat with gilded edges. A long metal staff was slung behind his back. At its tip were four pillars, where an orb crackled with mana-filled energy and snaps of lightning.

Over the mage's shoulder was the entrance to his home: scrolls strewn on the floor, beakers full of murky liquid substances, shelves and shelves of old archaic books full of lost knowledge.

"So you're going to gape at me and my stuff then?" sighed the Rorn. "Is that why you're here?"

He crossed his arms and peered at me with his faded blue eyes. There were lines all across his face. The man was tired and grumpy. Of the five different races Arondale's practicing mage had to be, it had to be the kind who hated the Aeri's guts. I really needed to put more attribute points into Luck.

"No I'm here because," I stammered. My voice cracked. I was nervous. Theobold had the air of the professors I'd had at college; the ones who listened to you with so much precision it made you uncomfortable to go on. I don't think he meant it in a bad way, it was who he was. He was serious. The words finally came to me and I said them: "I'd like to become a mage."

The tiniest quiver of a smirk appeared on Theobold's face.

"Oh really," he said. "What makes you think you have what it takes? Do you know any magic?"

Now it was my turn to smirk. "Actually, *I do*."

I closed my eyes and gathered all the energy inside myself and funneled it to the palm of my hand. I held up the glowing orb of light and power in front of Theobold and shot the ball out into the clear blue sky.

Theobold nodded his head, satisfactorily. "Good. Basic internal mana manipulation. What else can you show me?"

Wait—a goddamn energy ball wasn't enough to impress this

guy!? I scratched the back of my head and nervously said: "Um, actually, that's all I know. I hoped you would teach me more."

The old Rorn shook his head. He uncrossed his arms and slid them into the pockets of his coat. "I cannot teach you anything until you discover the basic skills that exist inside of you. Only then can we truly discuss you becoming a mage."

I slumped my shoulders and stared at the ground, the dirt welcoming me in my defeat. I wanted to blame the racial penalty. All Rorn hated Aeri. But I didn't think that had anything to do with it. I was missing something.

A window appeared in my HUD:

> *New Quest Alert: The Magic Inside of You!*
> *Discover the hidden abilities hiding within you. Maybe the Aeri in the Forgotten Forest nearby can help. Learn your main innate racial abilities (1/3)*
> *Quest Type: Uncommon*
> *Quest Difficulty: Hard*
> *Reward: 100 EXP + ?*
> *Accept: Yes/No ?*

I nodded my head, eagerly accepting the quest. The 100 EXP sounded nice but I was really in it for the question mark. It had to be related to unlocking the Apprentice Mage quest chain. I checked the time on my HUD. This was taking longer than I expected. I still had about another two hours before I met Serena. Did I have enough time? I wasn't sure. But I would keep pursuing it until I ran out. At that point I would use the waypoint teleportation system straight back to Arondale.

I was about to thank Theobold for pointing me in the

right direction but as I opened my mouth, the door
slammed shut right in my face.

17

The Forgotten Forest was a dark shrouded wood lying beyond the corn and wheat fields of west Arondale's farmland. I cut across a path, heading towards the forest. Halfway there, I stopped and had a picnic on the ground. I pulled a jar of honey and an apple out of my bag. Next I cut the apple into wedges with my sword. I then dipped the wedges into the jar of honey. The taste of sweet deliciousness took over me as a prompt appeared in my HUD:

You have discovered a new recipe: Honey Drenched
Apple Slices
Ingredients: Apple, Jar of Honey
A perfect afternoon snack. +3% faster HP regeneration
while in combat (Duration: 30 minutes)
Your cooking skill increased by 0.3.

Oh wow—it clearly paid off to eat your fruits and vegetables. What an awesome recipe. Extra HP regeneration was a potential life-saver. It would be great to discover a recipe with MP regeneration as well. Cooking was proving to be a very useful craft so far. Plus, as with last night, I felt way better after eating. I wasn't a teenager in my parent's basement anymore; ten hour binge sessions online needed to be broken up with meals.

I finished my snack, got back on my feet, and continued towards the Forgotten Forest. The different trees with their thick trunks and gnarled branches shadowed over me as I got near and approached the edge of the woods. It reminded me of the forest I'd been in yesterday with Shade, scrambling through the giant roots in search of a safe refuge after a traumatic evening. This wasn't those same woods but it brought back fresh memories.

Strange noises surrounded me the deeper I went into the forest. Sticks cracked. Bushes rustled. Unseen creatures snorted in the shadows. After a few minutes of walking, I turned around. No way. The passage by which I had come had all but disappeared.

Teeth chomped and swallowed something nearby. My head swerved. I unsheathed my sword and flexed my fingers, getting ready to charge an energy blast. I got on my knees, triggering the stealth ability, and poked my head from behind a bush. A small raptor with black skin and hard pink scales running down its forehead to its tail bent over a dead boar lying in a pool of blood. Flies hovered over the fallen beast.

The dinosaur perked up, revealing its head and long snout full of tiny razor sharp teeth. It was clearly a young raptor yet it already had a mouth wide enough to gobble my entire head. Blood dripped from its mouth. Its yellow eyes sought more prey to feast upon.

I took in the information available off its caption:

Raptor Hatchling
Level 10

I backed away. Level 10! Last time I went up against monsters with a significant level advantage I had nearly died. Correction: I *had* died. I had to get away from this raptor hatchling. I hated to think what its full-grown mother was like. I took a step backwards, my boot snapping on a twig. My stealth buff disappeared in an instant.

The raptor hatchling's eyes darted in my direction. Its mouth opened wide, the blood of the forest boar still dripping from its lips. Its long pink tongue stretched out and licked the crimson liquid off its teeth.

The creature took a step towards me.

"Alright now," I said. "Let's calm down."

I gripped my sword and readied myself for the baby dino's attack.

The raptor hatchling made a screaming war cry, hissing out blood and saliva. It charged at me. *Fuck this*. I ran. No way was I taking on a dinosaur, even a small one, in close combat.

I dashed through the trees, my heart thumping. Its clawed feet tapped against the ground as it chased after me. I made a quick turn around a large tree and charged up an energy ball and let it out, hitting the dinosaur in the stomach. I did about 20 HP of damage which took off a small sliver from its HP bar.

The attack only enraged the hatchling more. It wailed at me again and came towards me, mouth wide open, ready to chomp my arm off. I rolled out of the way and plunged my sword into its stomach. The raptor gave out a cry but the attack hardly did any damage. My energy ball was clearly the way to go. I needed to hit the creature in its critical spot, which clearly wasn't the creature's toughened rib cage.

Sharp teeth dug into my arm, tearing through my new apprentice coat and into my skin. The raptor jerked its head back, biting its teeth through my arm, attempting to rip it from my shoulder.

The initial bite took off 20 HP. This was better than I expected stat wise—clearly my new gear's bonuses to defense were making a difference—but the chomp hurt as bad as anything else. A bleeding debuff flashed on my HUD.

Bleeding (medium) (debuff): You have an open wound. You will lose 3 HP every thirty seconds. You cannot regenerate health until you stop bleeding.

I jabbed my sword in its ribs over and over until eventually the raptor let its teeth out of my flesh and jumped back. I powered up another energy ball right as it opened its mouth wide and came at me. I fired the energy ball directly into the creature's mouth. The creature swallowed the ball of light until a large implosion happened within the raptor's stomach, the outside of its ribs ballooning.

Critical hit!

The raptor fell to the floor as its HP bar fell below half. It wasn't dead, but my attack had crippled it. I think it was suffering from internal bleeding or broken bones. My energy blast had delivered a shockwave and tremor through its insides. Tears welled up in the creature's eyes as it stood on its legs only to collapse back on the ground.

I approached it, charging up another energy ball. The

dinosaur's eyes went red and it jumped onto its feet. The sudden movement made me accidentally shoot my energy ball off into the trees. Damn—what a waste of MP. The creature was deranged. Was it going to mutate like the Skren bandit had? No. Its plummeting HP had triggered a last resort rage mode. It was ready to fight for its life. Kill or be killed.

I sprinted away from the enraged raptor while charging up another energy ball. One more critical hit in the esophagus was all I needed. I spun around to face the incoming dinosaur. Its mouth was wide open and I shot the ball at it. The dinosaur clamped its mouth shut and knocked the energy ball out of its way with its snout, taking barely any damage.

Oh shit.

The propulsion of my own energy blast had forced me to fall to the ground. Now the dinosaur loomed over me, stumbling its wrecked body towards me. I had enough MP for three more energy balls. Then I was done. Dead. Game over.

I let the mana soak up in my palms, the glowing orb growing stronger and stronger as the dinosaur stretched its neck out. It was evaluating me like a food critic, deciding which part of me would be tastiest to bite into. It opened its mouth, teeth on full display as well as the dark pit which led to its stomach. I fired off the energy ball but the dino knocked it away with his snout again. Even in its frenzy, the creature had smartened up. It wouldn't be fooled by the same old trick again.

Still, I powered up another ball. If I shot it off fast enough, it wouldn't expect it. But nope. It knocked it away.

Fuck. I only had one chance left.

The raptor was licking its lips and swaying its head, entranced by the potential feast my body would offer him.

I gripped my sword and lunged forward. The raptor whacked the side of my blade with its own head. The blow overpowered me and sent me stumbling to the ground.

It opened its mouth for a quick bite. I lunged my free hand forward, delivering my fingers into the jaws of the beast. My arm got sticky and wet as the monster's teeth dug into my skin. Blood oozed from my flesh. As my HP plummeted, getting nerve-rackingly close to zero, I formed an energy ball in the very hand being chewed upon. I unleashed the blast right inside the monster's throat.

Critical Hit!

The creature's body exploded, flesh blasting out on the trees and drenching the shrubs in red. The monster's teeth slackened out of my flesh as the head slid off my arm.

+350 EXP!

Congratulations you have leveled up!
You gain +4 HP
You gain +1 MP
You have (3) unused attribute points that can be applied to any of your five base stats.

My HP and MP replenished to full. My wounds disappeared though my new coat remained patchy and damaged, especially on the one arm where I'd been bitten. I'd have to get it repaired. Wearers of light armor really weren't meant to solo this world. The material wasn't made for physical attacks, especially of the flesh-eating variety.

I approached the dead raptor and scanned it for items:

New Item(s) Alert!
Baby Dino Bone (x1)
Slab of Raptor Meat (x1)

My mouth watered at the cooking potential of the raptor meat. The bone would be great for brewing my own stock as well. I dug through the remains and took the loot and popped it in my inventory.

Catching my breath, I applied my newly acquired attribute points to my stats. I had been going too intensely with putting points into Magic Attack Power, so I'd spread them out more this level. I put one in spirit, pumping my total MP to 30. Now from the start of battle I was guaranteed six energy balls. MP regeneration usually added at least one more. I was sick of having so little HP, so I put one point into Toughness, which gave me an additional 5 health. I put my last point in my favorite stat: Magic Attack Power. More than anything else, that energy ball had saved me in the fight with the raptor. I looked over my stats, feeling pretty pleased.

Clay Hopewell
Level: 5
Race: Aeri (Eldra)
Class: N/A

HP: 116
MP: 30

ATKP: 3
MTKP: 30
TGH: 5
SPIRIT: 21

LUCK: 3

I sheathed my sword. Where had I ended up? Trees went on for days in every direction. I didn't understand how I was supposed to find the Aeri in here.

I continued to search the forest, admiring its beauty: from the old ancient trees to the beautiful exotic flowers. A large mushroom grew out from the ground beside a tree trunk. It had a big red shell and a beige stem. More crafting materials? I unsheathed my sword and approached the mushroom. As I crouched down and brought my knife to the bottom of the stem, it made a noise:

"Agh!"

I jumped back. Small arms sprouted out from the stem of the mushroom along with legs. What the--? A wrinkled craggy face emerged in the stem of the mushroom.

Mushroom Monster
Level 7

I charged an energy ball and blasted it at the monster. I did about 25 damage and took a nice chunk out of the monster's HP. The hit made it confused until it screamed and ran at me. Weirdly it stopped a meter in front of me. I didn't understand its movement pattern. What was it doing? It bent over, its whole body shaking, until purple vapor oozed out of its body from all directions. Next the mushroom monster sucked in a huge breath. Then it blew out a cloud of purple smoke towards me. A debuff flashed in my HUD.

Poisoned (Debuff): You have been poisoned! You lose 2

HP per 3 seconds until poison wears off (Duration: 1 minute)

40 HP gone in a minute so long as I didn't get hit by the poisoned smoke again and the debuff didn't stack. The mushroom monster at this point ran away. I chased after it until I realized—the clever monster bastard—wanted me to run through the smoke again. I backed off and ran around the plume of smoke until I had a clear running shot at the mushroom monster. He crouched down and prepared for launching another poison spray attack.

I charged straight at him and lunged my sword at the top of its mushroom head. It lost focus, disabling the poison spore attack. It wobbled back towards its original cloud of smoke, seeking shelter there. But even the spray had dwindled. I charged up an energy ball and whipped it at him. He cried out as his HP decreased. The cloud of smoke disappeared completely and I ran up to the monster and held it down with my leather boot. It bit into my foot, taking off a piece of HP every second it gnawed its teeth into my flesh. I alternated between stabbing and shooting, again and again until finally I charged up my final energy ball and sent the creature to its death.

+245 EXP!

Congratulations you have leveled up!
You gain +4 HP
You gain +1 MP
You have (3) unused attribute points that can be applied to any of your five base stats.

This forest was driving me mental but at least I got good

leveling and grinding from it. I quickly put all three attribute points into Magic Attack Power and did a quick scan of the mushroom monster, acquiring a "Batch of Mushrooms (x1) to add to my inventory and crafting supplies.

I marched through the forest.

"Hello!" I yelled.

I passed more mushrooms. I left them alone and they did the same for me. I was done with the grinding. I'd been attacked by baby dinosaurs and mushroom creatures and I was sick of it. When it came to battling creatures in this forest, there was no end in sight. I was ready to continue my quest. Find the Aeri.

Off in the darkness of the trees, a flicker of light appeared. Somebody giggled. It pierced my ears. The tiny hint of laughter made my ears twitch like a bug buzzing right in the lobe. Out of nowhere appeared a tiny green girl with clear butterfly wings. She waved at me and then planted herself right on the bridge of my nose.

My HUD read her caption:

Forest Pixy
Level 9

It wasn't antagonistic. I didn't want to attack it if I didn't have to.

The pixy giggled as it wagged its feet. It then pulled something out of its pouch. What was it doing? It pulled out a handful of powder and threw a whole pile of it straight into my eyes.

I screamed as the pixy blinded me with its magic dust. Jerk. I'd kill it. I unsheathed my sword ready to do battle. I swung it manically, hoping to hit something. The giggling disappeared. Had I killed it? But it didn't make sense as I hadn't received a notification for the experience bonus. What was going on?

When my sight returned, I was surrounded by cloaked figures from all sides. Each and every one of them held a bow with arrows nocked, ready to penetrate my skull.

18

"Explain yourself intruder," spoke one of the cloaked rangers. She had a rough feminine voice.

I gently put down my sword, then stood and held my hands above my head.

"I seek the Aeri of this forest," I said. "I need help learning the innate skills of our people."

The bowmen pointed their weapons to the ground but the woman ranger—clearly the leader of this pack—wasn't so easily convinced. She kept her arrow pulled back between her fingers, the tight string of the bow ready to release.

"I don't trust you," said the woman. "What kind of Aeri doesn't know the skills he is born with?"

She had a good point. What excuses did I have? I was one the Chosen? I didn't want to make the situation more confusing. I then had an idea straight out of Shade's charm playbook.

"I was told to come here by Theobold the Rorn," I said. "From what I know Rorn are not known as great practitioners of magic. Yet, for whatever reason, he is. If someone such as he can exist, is it so hard to believe there is an Aeri who's never learned his powers?"

The cloaked female ranger removed her hood, revealing a silver haired Aeri woman with pale skin and purple eyes like my own. Her ears angled into sharp points passing through her hair. She walked towards me and said: "You speak wise words. Perhaps you aren't an imposter after all. Any friend of Theobold's is a friend to the Eldra Aeri of the Forgotten Forest."

Barter (Level Two) Success
You increased your bartering skills by 0.3

I assumed bartering would mostly be useful in terms of dealing with merchants, but negotiating your own survival was good too.

"My name is Kendara," said the female ranger. "Come with us. I must show you to my grandmother—the eldest of our clan. Follow me."

The ranger threw her hood back over her head and walked between the trees. The other rangers jumped in the air with a quick magical lightness reaching the high branches above. They followed Kendara, leaping from branch to branch, watching her every step, keeping an eye on the dangers of the forest below. I jogged to catch up with the ranger, stumbling over a large oak root in the process. As we trudged forward, this strange sensation overtook me: it was the clarity and relief of heading in a constant direction after the madness of wandering in circles for far too long.

"Is there a spell in this forest which keeps people from entering too deep?"

Kendara smiled beneath her hood. "You figured that out, huh? The Eldra Aeri of the Forgotten Forest don't interact very much with the rest of Laergard. We leave outsiders to their concerns, we stick to ours."

Kendara's words confused me.

"You keep saying you're Eldra Aeri—but I thought they all lived on the continent of Orenspar?"

"All of the first Aeri were born in Orenspar—but that was a long time ago. Before the great rupture separated us all apart. The Eldra Aeri are those Aeri who stick to the old ways and traditions of the forest and the mother tree Gaia. No matter what continent they may live on."

There were so many blurred lines between the different races and factions, it was hard to keep track. At my next spare moment, I had serious research to do on the Wiki.

"But as you were saying about the forest's spell," said Kendara, as I followed behind her through a large shadowy crack in a tree. "Without one of us as a guide, you'd never be able to find Florentis."

"What the heck is Flor—"

Kendara stepped through a crack at the bottom of an ancient tree and disappeared. I followed behind and, like a portal, the forested doorway led to a magnificent town made of tree forts and humongous flowers. We stood on a tree root the size of a normal road which led to the center of the town. There large orange and purple petals rolled out like tongues, offering stairways to different buildings and sections of the town. Everything in the place had a glow to it, from the flowers, to the vines and roots we walked on. I guess this was an alternative form of lighting from the manatech I'd seen back in Arondale.

The Aeri walked to and fro throughout the city. There were all sorts of craftsmen busy at work: carving bows out of elder wood, reigniting the innate mana in dulled magic stones, inscribing swords with powerful scripts. I imagined the Eldra Aeri's economy here was mostly self-sufficient, but I bet they also imported a lot of basic goods and sold them back to the Haeren and other races after being magically inscribed and improved upon. Aeri children ran about, sliding down flower petals, laughing with glee.

What a beautiful place.

You've discovered Florentis! +100 EXP!

"Come with me odd Aeri man," said Kendara. "I must take you to my grandmother. The rest of you are dismissed."

The cloaked group of rangers nodded and all walked away. A group of them headed to a flower petal where there was a fountain of bright green liquid. Other Aeri sipped on the drink from wooden tankards. An Aeri tavern.

Kendara walked down the large root road to the center of the city where a long green stem shot out of the ground and through the canopy of the trees. A vine staircase wound around the stem. Kendara walked up and, after a few steps, paused to glare at me waiting at the bottom, hesitancy written across my face.

"Don't tell me you've spent so long in the Haeren realms you're weary of our architecture? Does everything really need to be stone and concrete to make you feel comfortable?"

This elf girl was throwing me pretty hardcore shade so I played it cool and said, "Sorry, my mind slipped. I got no problem with flower stairs."

She rolled her eyes. She knew I was bullshitting but I think she enjoyed my failed attempt at coolness.

I followed behind her until we were atop all the flower

buildings and the glowing Aeri town laid below. It was stunning and so different from the industrial and polluted Arondale. We passed through the branches and trees until we were above the entire forest. The bright blue sky surrounded us. Theobold's windmill and the shadowy silhouette of Arondale stood in the distance like tiny specks. The vine staircase led us to a yellow tulip the size of a house.

"Hang on a second," I said. "I didn't see this tower when I approached the forest."

"Of course you didn't. Just like you were unable to find your way around the place until we approached you. Old and powerful magic courses through this forest. How else would we protect ourselves from those who seek to exploit the forest's magic?"

Kendara shook her head. The thought of outsiders really did bother her.

She continued forward. The vine led us directly inside the flower, where the large petals acted like walls. Light from the late morning sky floated through the slivers between the petal walls. An old Aeri woman sat cross-legged in the center of the room, her eyes were closed.

The old Aeri opened her eyes. They were faded and lavender in color. She had wrinkled skin and silver hair braided into a weaving pony-tail far longer than her.

"Grandma," said Kendara. "I found a stranger in the woods. He appears Aeri like you or me but—"

"He doesn't act like an Aeri at all," the old woman finished her granddaughter's sentence.

"Exactly!" Kendara said, excitedly. "Grandma—how did you know?"

"The forest speaks to me child," said the old woman. "It speaks, and I listen. There will be more like them soon. The *Gaia-Rentha* is at hand."

I stepped forward. "Are you talking about the Chosen?"

The old woman shook her head and smiled. "The Haeren—so arrogant. Everything is about me, me, me. Yes—we are talking about the Chosen. Or as we call it, *Gaia-Rentha*: Gaia gives birth. New beings are entering our world, marking a new age. Gaia tells us it is so."

"So you'll accept me as an Aeri like you guys?"

Both women laughed. "You are a Haeren dressed up as an Aeri. Everyone can see."

Geeze—these guys were perceptive beyond belief. I worried they'd start talking about Earth and Taco Bell in a minute.

"Okay, but will you teach me our innate abilities," I asked. I created an energy ball in my hand. "I can already do this one."

The two woman made a face at one another, impressed.

"Kendara here can teach you what you wish to learn," said the elder Aeri woman. "But on one condition. A certain set of mushrooms have become plagued and threaten to poison the whole forest. If you help Kendara eradicate the pest, you will learn the full set of innate skills. Are you up to the task?"

Quest Update: The Magic Inside of You

You have successfully met the Eldra Aeri of the Forgotten Forest. Help them in clearing the woods of the plagued mushroom creatures and discover the innate abilities currently locked within you. Learn your main innate racial abilities (1/3). Destroy the mushroom plague threatening the forest
Quest Type: Uncommon
Quest Difficulty: Hard

Reward: 100 EXP + ?
Accept: Yes/No ?

I accepted the quest straightaway, though I shivered at the thought of going back into the forest full of dangerous dinosaurs and haunted mushrooms.

19

A message appeared in my HUD: *Kendara has joined your party*. Underneath my status bars and debuff icons, a picture of Kendara's face appeared. I focused on her image to get all of her stats.

Kendara
Level 8
Race: Aeri (Eldra)
Class: Ranger

HP: 118
MP: 24

ATKP: 22
MTKP: 3
TGH: 14
SPIRIT: 18
LUCK: 7 (+2)

I pored over her stats to take in her build. She was a nice

mix of all the base stats except when it came to magic attack power which surprised me given how so much of the Eldra Aeri skill set involved one's innate mana flow. I was curious to see her in battle.

We said goodbye to the Aeri elder and headed back down the vine to the main level of Florentis. I headed for the exit when Kendara frowned at me.

"You always go into battle like this?"

There were ripped holes and tears in my dirty coat. I called up the stats and saw the durability was close to 0.

"You're right, I better get this repaired before we head off and deal with those mushroom monsters."

Kendara motioned with her hands, telling me to follow her. We walked up a petal of a glowing green flower, leading to a hall of Aeri, busy working at different crafting stations from forges to tanning racks. The ranger led me to one man, specifically. He was a young Aeri with blonde hair and he was sewing together a cloth. Faint light emanated from his fingertips onto the needle and thread as he infused it with internal mana.

"Clarex—can you repair this for us quickly?"

I took my coat off and handed it to the young boy. He picked it up in his hands and smiled as he stitched it using the same mana-infused sewing he had done earlier. Within a minute, the coat was as good as new.

I donned my newly repaired coat and Kendara was back to business. "Time to get going. The forest plague grows stronger every minute we waste."

Kendara led the way and we exited Florentis back through the forest portal, appearing outside the ancient tree.

"Which way?" I asked.

"We'll travel faster and see more if we travel by tree branch," said Kendara.

"Wait, what?"

Kendara jumped off the ground and—rather than falling back down—she simply jumped in the air again. She did this three times and then landed onto the branches of the gnarled trees.

"Um," I said. "I don't think I can do that."

Kendara shook her head. "Of course you can. Try it."

I felt like an idiot because I knew I wasn't going to be able to do it. Not on the first try anyway. I jumped and kicked my feet higher in the air but all I did was fall on my ass. Kendara laughed from the branches.

"No, not like that," she said, holding her stomach in laughter. "You're going to make me fall off this branch." She wiped a tear out of her eye. "Think about it like this. When you summon the energy ball, you're focusing all the mana inside of you into your palm. Now when you try to jump, try focusing the mana on the bottom of your feet. Use the energy as a momentary platform to jump again."

I kind of understood what Kendara meant but not entirely. To fully comprehend her words, I needed to try. I bent my knees and jumped in the air. As I came back down, I focused on my feet, pushing the mana inside me downwards. An odd thick puddle platform rested beneath my feet, which wasn't quite the forest floor. I jumped again in excitement, straight into the bushes.

A window appeared in my HUD:

Innate Racial Ability Unlocked: *Power Jump (Level One)*
Manipulate the mana coursing inside of you to create platforms through which you jump higher and higher.
MP Cost: 7

"I've learnt the ability," I yelled up to Kendara, excitedly.

"You've learnt it when you're up here on this branch with me. Focus your mana to your feet as soon as you jump. It's too late once you're already falling back down."

Okay. This was it. I would do it right this time. I had to focus. It was a split-second thing. I had to be powering up my feet as soon as I jumped—not quite before and not even a second after. It had to be immediate.

I crouched down, wanting to put all my strength in my knees for this. I lunged my body forward, my feet pushing off the ground. I let the mana course through them and, sensing the platform below, I jumped again. I was in the middle of the air—between the forest floor and the branches above. It was like flying until I fell—*oh no*. I created another energy puddle and jumped and did it once more until I clung to the branch.

Kendara held her hand out for me and pulled me up.

Standing upright on the branch, I wiped the sweat off my forehead. Close call. If I hadn't made it to the branch in those last two hops, I would've been out of MP and would've fallen back to the ground.

Note to self: at full MP I had enough for four power jumps. Otherwise, splat. I'm sure if I used it enough, I would level up the skill and the MP cost would go down.

"Well done," she said. "With enough practice, you'll fool me into believing you're a normal Aeri." She then turned her head and pointed in the direction of other branches. "Follow me. We'll hop between the branches, scouring the forest for these plagued mushroom monsters."

Kendara moved forward and jumped into open space, creating a platform of energy at her feet, and jumped to the next branch. I followed behind her. We took time between branches scouting the forest floor, letting our MP recharge.

After about ten minutes of branch hopping, Kendara stopped and fell into a stealthy crouch. She put her hand out to stop me from moving.

"Down there," she whispered. "Big enough patch to spread the plague."

Below us was a cluster of five purple mushrooms. They appeared innocuous like the red mushrooms I'd fought earlier. But of course, it was their disguise.

"What should we do?" I asked. At five versus two, the odds were in their favor. We did have an advantage of height though.

"I'll hop over to the branch on the other side," said Kendara. "I'll rain down arrows while you blast out energy balls. We will take them out with ease. Follow my lead." She hopped over to the tree on the other side of the mushroom patch. The ranger pulled out an arrow from her satchel on her back and nocked the arrow in her bow. Her arrow took on a silky luminescence. It was a coating of her own mana. She released the magic arrow, landing a critical hit on the central mushroom. Purplish blood spurt out of the creature's head.

The mushrooms sprouted out of the ground, angry faces appearing on their stems. Their captions came into view. All the same.

Plagued Mushroom Monster
Level 8

I charged up an energy ball and whipped it down towards the group of mushrooms. It hit two of them, dishing out damage to both. Kendara kept a steady stream of silver arrows flying down to the patch of unsuspecting mushrooms. Puddles of purple blood filled the forest floor. It was a fungi massacre.

I didn't realize how powerful our height advantage was; focusing on the same targets. We killed two of the mushrooms straight away. Experience prompts stacked in my HUD and I even got a notification for leveling up. I waved the information away.

The three remaining plagued mushroom monsters all crouched beside each other. Uh oh. The purple smoke oozed out of their bodies, filling the forest area in a poisonous mist. The three of them created such a thick cloud of smoke, it hid them and shielded them from our blasts.

"Keep firing," said Kendara, as the purple smoke billowed higher into the air, approaching us on the branches. The poison debuff prompt appeared on my screen.

Poisoned (Debuff): You have been poisoned! You lose 2 HP per 3 seconds until poison wears off (Duration: 1 minute)

I ignored the debuff and kept charging up energy balls and throwing them below. But none of our hits landed.

The three mushrooms gathered around the tree. All three of them placed their hands on its trunk. The wood slowly turned purple and the branch I stood on sagged beneath my weight, the whole trunk shaking. I had barely enough MP to hop across the open air to Kendara's branch. The tree toppled and crashed to the forest floor, making a massive tremor. Dirt rippled through the ground as the roots of the tree were pulled out and left off to the side.

"We have to jump down there and fight them up close," I

said. "Otherwise they'll keep plaguing the trees and we won't even have a forest to save in the end."

"Alright, stay close, and we'll focus on one target at a time."

She jumped down making a small platform for herself right near the edge of the forest floor to cushion her fall. I followed suit and unsheathed my sword. I'd have to fight with it as my mana replenished.

I ran through the poison mist as Kendara's silver arrows flew past me into the eyeball of one of the mushroom creatures. I stabbed it with my sword. I swiped one way and then another, slowly chipping away at its health.

The three mushroom creatures surrounded me. A fungi fist smashed right into my face, followed by a swarm of kicks to my legs. I squirmed and lifted my arms in defense. I kept close track of my MP but I still didn't have enough to fire off another energy ball. Then I remembered the MP potion in my bag. I multitasked: swiping my sword in self-defense as I scrolled through my HUD opening my inventory window and selecting MP potion. The glass bottle of blue liquid materialized in my hand. I yanked out the cork and guzzled the potion down. Mana replenished, I charged up an energy ball and blasted it into the weakest mushroom's face, shooting fungi flesh onto the neighboring trees.

+280 EXP!

With the opening, I rolled out of the way. I was below 50% HP and the poison debuff was nearly over. But I toggled through my buffs and saw the duration still ran at 1 minute. What the hell--? It's because the mist still hasn't cleared, meaning as long as I stood in the mist, the poison duration didn't go down. I received a renewed debuff of poison every time I breathed.

I ran out of the purple cloud and joined Kendara from where she was firing her arrows. The mist had faded enough so our enemies were visible.

"Let's fire all we got from here," I said. "Let's get them before they unleash another plume of smoke."

Kendara shot her silver arrows and I charged up energy balls. I made sure to knock the mushrooms before they let out their poison gas. They waddled towards us, but working together on one mushroom at a time, we made quick work of them.

+280 EXP!
+280 EXP!

Congratulations you have leveled up!
You gain +4 HP
You gain +1 MP
You have (6) unused attribute points that can be applied to any of your five base stats

I toggled to my stat screen and threw 3 points into spirit and another 3 points into magic attack power. Next I ran over to the plagued mushrooms to see if they had any loot. I acquired a crafting a material I didn't see myself using anytime soon. *Batch of Poisoned Mushrooms (x4).*

"Do you think we got the source of it all?" I asked Kendara.

She shook her head. "These purple headed mushrooms can be found all over. We need to find the source of where the plague is coming from."

The ground beneath us trembled. It cracked into jagged

lines of dirt. A horrible smell infected the whole surrounding area. Kendara and I backed away from the swelling forest floor.

"Get ready," said Kendara.

Emerging from out of the ground was a mushroom the size of a large elephant. It had a purple head with glowing green dots. It had angry red eyes and a million tiny razor sharp teeth. It shadowed over us as I read the caption:

[Plagued Mushroom Lord].

20

"How the hell do we fight this thing?"

I shivered at the sight of the horrible fungus monster. The others had been small and freaky but this guy was really awful. Green gas oozed out of the holes in its cap. It waddled around the surrounding patch of forest in a dazed stupor. Its arms and legs were shriveled and grey like withered branches. It headed towards us.

"We can't let it unleash a vapor spray like its minions," said Kendara. "Not only will it kill us, but it will destroy whole sections of the Forgotten Forest." She nocked an arrow and let it glimmer with shiny silver light and launched it at the beast, hitting it in the stem. Its health bar lowered.

It crouched down and I worried it was preparing a poison spray attack, so I charged up an energy ball and blasted it at the creature. It did pittance for damage and it didn't do anything to knock the creature back. The magical blast bothered it immensely though. I prepared myself for a cloud of poisonous smoke but the mushroom lord did something different. It leapt in the air and came flying at me, mouth wide open with a million tiny pincer teeth.

I jumped backwards, created a mana platform and jumped again to dodge the attack. Holy shit. An instant death attack for sure.

Kendara strafed away and continued to fling arrows at it, whittling away at its HP. If she continuously shot at the creature unbothered, it would take awhile but we'd be able to kill it.

"Kendara," I yelled to her as I dodged another leap attack from the mushroom lord. "Get onto the branches above and keep firing at it. I'll keep it distracted as you whittle it away."

She nodded her head and leapt to the canopy above. Meanwhile the mushroom lord kept hobbling towards me, eager to see me destroyed. I powered up an energy ball and shot it right at its eye.

Blocked!

What the hell? Its magical defense was through the roof. My fingers fidgeted around the hilt of my sword. My ATKP wasn't high enough to deal much damage. It would be an extreme risk to get up close and personal with it. But what were our other options?

It bellowed and rampaged towards me. How did it become so fast? I turned around and ran. Kendara's arrows swished past me, slicing through the air, knocking off bits of flesh of the monster. I had to keep running, keep the thing distracted until we killed it. It wasn't the most valorous way to win a fight. But we weren't fighting for valor now, were we?

I ran through the forest, hearing the stomping tremors of the mushroom lord behind. It squashed shrubs and bushes as it charged through the forest. My throat burned. My heart raced.

I darted past a large tree and spun around it, hoping to confuse the mushroom lord. Gaining a few meters on it, I stopped and sent an energy ball at its face. It still had over half of its HP left.

Kendara's arrows shot down through the branches, creating open wounds on the mushroom lord, purple blood spurting out of him.

"Clay—we need to kill it faster," yelled Kendara from up above. "The gas coming out of its head will only further corrupt the forest."

I yelled to the branches above. "My energy ball doesn't do any damage to it. I don't know what to do."

"Use your sword!"

"What do you mean?" I said, panting as I ran away from the mushroom lord's charge. "I'm weakest with my sword!"

"Infuse it with your mana," she said. "Try it."

I unsheathed my sword and as I ran I let the mana inside of me course up to my hand and next I let it spill out onto my sword. A silver glow enveloped my rapier. I stopped, enthralled by its beauty.

Innate Racial Ability Unlocked: *Mana Infusion*
(Level One)
Manipulate the mana coursing inside of you to render other objects (weapons, armor, etc.) more powerful

Skill Type: Mana-Based
MP Cost: 5

I would study the new skill more closely later. Right now, I had to fight.

I spun around with my new silvery sword and swung the blade at the incoming Mushroom Lord. I drove a gash through it, chipping off thirty HP. The new magical sword must be combining both my ATKP and MTKP into a stronger attack. Wicked.

The creature slashed with its gnarled hands, scratching me across the chest. The pain rippled through me. Half of my HP dropped off in an instant. *Fucking shit*—when was I going to party up with a tank already? My build wasn't meant to handle these kinds of hits.

I turned around and ran from the mushroom lord. I grabbed my health potion from my inventory and guzzled it down, returning to full health. One hit from this monster and I was toast.

I power jumped onto the branches above me. I quickly hopped over to others until the mushroom lord lost track of me. Kendara continued to shoot at the giant mushroom, attracting its hate onto her.

"Clay—what are you doing? This isn't the plan!"

The mushroom lord turned its back to me and I ran across the branch and jumped off, swinging a silvery mana infused sword above my head, and dragging it downward on top of the mushroom lord, stabbing the monster with all my energy and force. I drained all my MP into the sword as it dug deeper and deeper into the mushroom lord's skull. A long list of critical hits came one after the other until the giant mushroom collapsed like a deflated balloon onto the forest floor.

+455 EXP!

Congratulations you have leveled up!
You gain +4 HP
You gain +1 MP
You have (3) unused attribute points that can be applied
to any of your five base stats.

I walked away from the fallen creature and fell back against a nearby tree in exhaustion. Kendara jumped down from the branches, breaking her fall with a mana platform.

"Do you feel it?" she said. She raised her hands above her head, twirling her fingers in the air. "The forest is healing. We destroyed the source of the forest's plague!"

I nodded my head. I was happy the battle with the mushroom lord was over.

"We must go speak to my grandmother of this fortunate news at once," said Kendara. She walked over to me and stuck out her hand to help me out. "When I first met you, Clay Hopewell, I thought you were an imbecile, a disgrace to the Aeri lineage. But I now know I was wrong."

"Thanks, I guess."

We strolled through the Forgotten Forest in the direction of Florentis. The forest glowed with a new vivacity. I was happy to see it returned to normal health.

When we got back to Florentis, we went straight to Kendara's grandmother at the the tulip tower above the canopy.

"Grandmother," Kendara said when we arrived. "We succeeded at ridding the mushroom plague from the forest."

The old Aeri woman nodded. "I know child; I sensed the plague relinquishing its stranglehold on the life of the forest as soon as you defeated the mushroom lord. Yet," the woman's voice took on a hushed tone. "There's a darkness encroaching the surrounding area. An ancient evil. I can sense it. It won't be long until it affects those of us in this forest."

Was she speaking about the mutated creatures?

Her voice returned to normal: "Thank you, Clay Hopewell, for assisting us."

A prompt appeared in my HUD:

You have successfully completed Quest: The Magic Inside of You!
+100 EXP!

You have gained status amongst the Eldra Aeri faction of the Forgotten Forest (Eastern Laergard). You have gone from "positive" to "respected" status.

"For your aid, please accept this gift from the people of Florentis," said the old woman, and materializing in her arms was a long wooden mage's staff.

New Item Alert! Apprentice's Staff (ATKP: 15-20. MTKP: 20-40. REQ: 20 MTKP+)
Do you wish to add this to your inventory (Yes/No)?

I added the staff to my inventory. I was pumped to wield it.

"With that staff," explained the elder. "You'll now be able to draw mana from the world around you to help add extra power to your abilities."

Kendara approached me and said, "Thanks again Clay. Please return to Florentis soon, so we can go hunting and," she smiled, "I can teach you more ways to be a proper Aeri." She then leaned over and planted a kiss on my cheek.

Any regrets I had for picking Aeri as my starting race vanished in an instant.

21

The time on my HUD said it was 12:50 p.m. Oh shit. I had ten minutes to get back to Arondale and meet Serena. For a brief second, I had a mild panic attack: I'm not going to make it back in time, Serena is going to think I'm a massive dickhead and disappear to another part of Illyria never to be seen again.

I sighed with relief when I remembered the ability to travel between waypoints. But I would need to get some gold first. I headed down the vine staircase and sold my newly acquired loot to an Aeri merchant, gaining hopefully enough money for the waypoint transfer.

Next I thought *world map* and the vision in my HUD was taken over by a transparent map of Illyria. Most of the map was fuzzy, only revealing the contours of the massive continents. When I focused on Laergard, the map grew clearer, revealing the small percentage of the world I had explored. A golden cursor represented where I was on the map and I moved my eyes to the right of there and found Arondale. I focused on Arondale; how do I trigger fast travel teleportation there?

Responding to my thoughts, a prompt appeared:

*Would you like to fast-travel to Arondale waypoint for 10
gold coins (Yes/No)?*

Yes, I said in my head and instantly I disintegrated into
dust. A few seconds later, I rematerialized in a market
square back in Arondale. My stomach lurched. My feet
wobbled, disorientated from the teleport travel. I patted my
cheeks down to my legs, making sure I was all still there.
The midday sun shined in my eyes as I took in the busy
streets. The market was throbbing with people—even more
than there had been in the morning. Adventurers walked by
with bowls of food, cooked fish wrapped in paper, and other
mouthwatering snacks.

Serena had said to meet in the church square. This city
was overflowing with squares and piazzas. I faintly recalled
Shade pointing a Haeren church out to me at the center of
town. The church's blue dome hovered over the rest of the
city and I headed towards it.

As I went down the streets, passing shopkeepers and
travelling merchants, Serena filled my thoughts: her long
brown hair she always kept tied in a ponytail and her silver
rimmed glasses, big and circular. It had been years since I
last saw her. She had been incredibly studious, so I imagined she was like me and had gone for a spellcaster class.
She would have tips on how to finally unlock the class.

I turned a corner, entering the church square. A massive
cathedral with a blue dome hung over me. I searched the
area for a fountain and saw a large stone watering hole with
a statue of a Haeren god standing between two different
planets. Above him was a stone vase on a column from

which water sprayed out in a glorious fall. There was only one person sitting at the fountain. A young woman. But I wasn't sure if it was Serena. The girl was clad in bright red bikini armor with a giant sword sheathed behind her back.

The woman jumped to her feet with a huge smile brightening her face. She ran up to me and practically tackled me with a hug. I almost fell back from the weight of her sword, but she held us both up. Her attack power stat—which effected one's muscular strength—must've been super high.

"It's so good to see you," she said.

"You too," I said, squeezing her tightly. I let go and found myself struggling for words. Where did I even start? Serena was the first person from home I was meeting here in this new world. All the frightening things on Earth—ZERO and its mutated form, the riots, the border shutdowns—rushed back to me, reminding me of how I ended up here. "If you're here, you were infected with the—"

"Shh," whispered Serena. "Let's not think about what brought us here. At least not yet. Let's be happy the two of us found each other."

She was right. Somehow I felt more at home, safer now with someone I knew. Someone I trusted. Being with Serena felt right. A deep pang of guilt came through my chest. What if I had stayed in college? What would have happened to us then? I shook the thought out of my mind. We were here now. Focus on the present.

She disentangled herself from me and held my shoulders, taking me in. "You're Aeri, huh? Most people go Haeren, you know."

"I wonder why," I said, half-attempting a joke. Serena shrugged at my lame attempt at humour. Call me Mr. Smooth.

"Have you unlocked your class yet? I can't tell. I was half-expecting you to be a Thief or Rogue character," she laughed. I guess dropping out of college and travelling around had left an impression of what kind of person I was.

"It's funny you say that. I never liked playing thief. Too much waiting around in the shadows. I liked the stealthy bits, but I found I got too impatient," I explained. "But yeah I'm working towards becoming an apprentice mage. This world is so incredible. It feels like I'm being offered a second chance, you know. Becoming a mage is a chance to be the student I had never been."

Serena let go of my shoulders and rubbed her earlobe with her right hand. It was so strange. A gesture she'd done all the time back in the real world. Here she was a whole new person in appearance, but underneath it all was still the girl I once knew.

"I know what you mean," she said. "I'm sorry for saying you'd be a thief. I'd have been annoyed if you'd assumed I was going to be a spell caster or something…"

"I'd never presume."

"…So I chose blade soldier as my class. Long story about the quest chain to unlock it. I'll tell you another time. But, exactly as you were saying, I wanted a second chance. I didn't want to be a mousy bookworm anymore. I wanted to be more outgoing, more forthright. I wanted to be someone who stands up for what they believe in. As soon as I arrived in Laergard: I knew. I felt it in me. I'd be a warrior, a fighter."

There was fire in her voice as she spoke.

"If you need my help achieving your goals Serena, I'm here to help," I said. "Plus, as a squishy glass cannon who can be killed in a hit or two, I really need to party up with a tank. I think we'd make a good team."

Serena smiled. "Good. I'm glad you feel that way. I was thinking the same thing. But I need to talk to you about something. Something big and—" Serena broke into tears.

I put my arm on her shoulder and said, "Tell me everything."

22

We sat down at the edge of the stone fountain and Serena told me everything she'd been holding back.

"I think there's something wrong with the game," she said. "I don't know what, but things are happening that aren't supposed to be happening. Mutations. Glitches. This world isn't as stable as TriCorp made it out to be."

"Serena—did anything happen to you?"

She shook her head. "No. But when I entered the game a few days ago, I spawned in a small village in the middle of the continent and something happened." She took a breath. "I watched a bunch of beginner players get rampaged by this pterodactyl monster. I wouldn't have thought anything of it but the creature's design didn't make any sense. There were arms festering out of it and parts of the body were fragmented and inverted. The creature was suffering from serious glitches. Next thing I knew it completely obliterated the players fighting it. They disappeared. I went around asking about them and no had seen them since. I don't think they ever respawned." Serena took a deep sigh and planted her hands on her knees. "Clay—I don't think you understand how scary it was. I'd been in the game less than a couple of hours—I was still getting used to this new reality —and when I saw that *thing*, I instantly knew it wasn't right. It was a mutation. The game's internal A.I. isn't working properly. It's horrible."

"Serena," I said. "I think I understand better than you realize." I pulled the gloves off and showed her the dark swirling mark on my wrist.

"What are you showing me?"

I told her the whole story. From spawning in the Skren caravan to fighting through the bandits to finally the fight with the mutated bandit leader.

"When I returned after death, I had this mark," I said. "I thought a quest prompt would appear but nothing of the sort has happened. The NPC innkeeper recognized it though. She's the one who gave me these gloves. Still, no one has told me what it means."

"That's awful Clay. As soon as I witnessed the mutated monster, I knew I had a purpose here in A.K.O. I was going to figure out what those things are and how to stop them. Seriously, if these glitches don't get put under control, NPCs and players alike will find ways to exploit them. Someone with such a level of power would be able to completely rewrite the rules of the game. We have to stop the spread of this problem before it goes any further."

"Have you contacted the TriCorp Dev team?"

"I wrote them last night and still haven't heard back. I feel like we have to deal with this problem from the inside."

I took a deep breath. Last night's dream came back to me. The face of the girl with pigtails. She had asked for help.

"Do you know anything about how dreaming works in the game?"

"So far I can't say I've had any. I don't want to say the sleep is instantaneous from one night to the next morning—but when I wake up, I can't recall any dreams. Could just be me though."

"Well listen to this: I had a dream last night. This girl was begging me for help. What if she's part of the game's A.I. as well? What if she's reaching out to me because she thinks I can help with the mutations?"

Serena shook her head. "There's too much we still don't understand. I don't even know where to begin."

"I have a quest about to start and I think it will lead us to more answers," I said. "The Knights of Laergard and—" I wasn't sure how to describe Shade. "This other guy are going on a search party for the mutated Skren leader. Do you want to party up?"

Serena smiled and then hesitated.

"What is it?"

"Yeah I want to party up," she said. "But, as you were telling your story, I noticed you said you'd only been in the game for a day. Does that mean—?"

There was still a looming possibility my mind would explode from sensory overload and I'd die, disappearing from this world and our old one altogether?

"Yes," I said. "Yes it does."

23

Serena and I partied up and I got a quick glimpse at her stats.

Serena Wharton

Level: 15
Race: Haeren (Laergardian)
Class: Blade Soldier

HP: 291
MP: 19

ATKP: 51
MTKP: 3
TGH: 32
SPIRIT: 3
LUCK: 3

She had a potent mix of melee attack strength plus

toughness, making her a good damage dealer as well as tank. Wicked.

"Hey—it's rude to ogle over someone's stats," Serena said, knocking me out of my HUD trance. "Didn't you say we had a quest to do."

"Right," I said, spinning around and heading into the throng of the market place towards the Royal Knights of Laergard's guild hall.

We hurried past the vendors and over the canal bridge and through the posh district, until we arrived in front of the guild outpost. Shade and Edward Silver stood outside, waiting for us. They made an odd pair: the loyal knight and the mischievous thief. I hoped no rumors tarnished Silver's reputation.

"You sure took your sweet time," said Shade, his tail wagging behind him. "Who's this?"

"This is my friend Serena," I said, introducing her to the others. "She's joining us for the quest."

Edward grunted. "A blade soldier? Really?"

Serena whispered in my ear. "This is a bad time to tell you but blade soldiers and royal knights don't get along very much. There's a strong rivalry between them. Two different military disciplines."

"I'm sure it will be fine so long as you don't kill us all with your ridiculous sword," said Edward.

"Alright enough bickering about who wields their sword better," said Shade. "Knight-man, tell them what you told me."

Edward's posture changed, signaling he had important information to tell us. "A band of travelling merchants arrived in town earlier and spoke of a foul creature heading in the direction of Golpe Swamplands. It sounds like the creature you described earlier. We should head there and investigate."

> **Quest Update: Mysterious Creature in the Woods**
> *Sightings of a deadly creature have been reported in the Golpe Swamplands. Head there and see what you can find.*
> *Quest Type: Unique*
> *Quest Difficulty: Hard*
> *Reward: 100 EXP + ?*

"Are you ready?" the knight asked. He regarded my rusty rapier with a grimace. "You might want to exchange your garden tool of a weapon for something more substantial. Head to the courtyard and take one of the extra swords on the weapon rack."

I shrugged off the captain's snide remarks. He was offering gear for free. Great deal in my book. I ran to the courtyard where there were still soldiers practicing their bayonet and shield work. A wooden rack of weapons stood off to the side against the cold walls of the courtyard. I scanned the items and saw the swords were all relatively the same.

> **New Item Alert!** *Basic Short Sword (ATKP: 20-25)*
> *Do you wish to equip (Yes/No)?*

I equipped the the new sword, letting the old rusty one dematerialize back into my inventory. I ran back to the group waiting outside and asked Serena, "How are you doing for potions?"

Serena shrugged. "I got a few and don't really have the gold coins to spare."

"Fair, fair," I said and then lifted my finger to tell the group, *give me one more second please.* I hurried down the road to the western gate and found the potion vendor was still standing there with her wheelbarrow full of potions. I sold her my rusty rapier for 13 gold coins and my baby dino bone for 4. I was up to 22 gold coins. I used almost everything I had buy an HP potion and MP potion each. I thanked the vendor and returned to the group.

"I'm ready," I said.

"Good," said Edward, appearing under my party icon along with Shade and Serena. "Let's head to the southern gate."

As we walked briskly through the afternoon streets of Arondale, I perused our new party member's stats.

Edward Silver

Level: 30
Race: Haeren (Laergardian)
Class: Royal Knight

HP: 550
MP: 39

ATKP: 47
MTKP: 3
TGH: 66
SPIRIT: 8
LUCK: 3

Holy shit! Level 30. Edward Silver was super strong. There were also all of his unseen stats and buffs on his gear. I bet it only doubled his strength and defenses. He was an incredibly tough tank. Exactly what we needed. I moved on from his stats and took in Shade's.

Shade
Level 4
Race: Lirana
Class: Thief

HP: 137
MP: 11

ATKP: 21
MTKP: 3
TGH: 14
SPIRIT: 4
LUCK: 36

Hmm. Shade hadn't leveled since our battle in the Skren encampment from the evening before. Why? How come some NPCs leveled up while others stayed on the lower end of the spectrum? It must come down to fighting monsters. Edward was a soldier so he fought in wars and gained loads of experience points. Meanwhile, Shade—a thief—wasn't necessarily going out and killing monsters, so his base stats wouldn't rise much. I bet, however, his stealth and thieving stats were phenomenally high as he practiced those skills. I guess it made sense in its own way. Most NPCs—villagers, merchants, every day folk living their lives—they didn't run around killing mobs all day like players did. No wonder their levels were low. They didn't even think in those terms.

"Are you drooling over stats again," chided Serena with a smile.

"No," I said. "I was looking over our party. We're quite

strong but I'm worried about Shade. He's a much lower level than the rest of us and unlike you or me, he won't come back to life if he dies."

"We'll have to keep an eye on him," said Serena. "But early leveling is quite quick in this game, so depending on the amount of mobs we fight on the way he will catch up to us fast."

The mana gate was wide open for easy passage when we got there. This was where Shade and I had first entered Arondale the previous evening. It was different during the day. Busier and friendlier. A closed guarded gate only projected fear and animosity.

We stepped through the passage and into the valley of farmer's fields and windmills. Edward and Shade walked ahead while Serena and I marched behind them.

"So Shade is the NPC you fought those Skren bandits with?" Serena asked.

"Yeah," I said. "Why do you ask?"

"I'm curious, that's all. Most NPCs don't usually stick around after a quest has failed. They definitely don't break from your party and meet with you later to continue a highly dangerous quest. Impressive, Clay. The fact this guy is returning means he's bonded to you somehow. Surviving the Skren kidnapping has brought you two together. He respects you now."

I had never really thought about it. Shade and respect didn't really go hand in hand; at least not with regards to things people *usually* respected: like authority, the law, other people's boundaries. Shade never struck me as someone capable of such noble emotions. But maybe I've judged him too quickly. Maybe he's actually my friend. The first one I had made in this world.

We passed the farms and headed up the hill towards the forest, the same one Shade and I had traversed the previous evening. With my new sword sheathed at my waist and my apprentice staff strapped to my back, I was ready to test my new weapons out on enemy mobs, but the forest was all but empty when we arrived. We hurried through the shadows, but nothing was present. A wild doe hurried away from us. It was smart enough to sense a battle would be its death sentence.

I admired the surroundings of the forest as we strolled through it: the gnarled oak trees, the pine needles on the floor, the chirping and pretty birds fluttering between the branches. The soft strands of sunlight poking through the canopy of trees. It was so hard to believe this was all a game. A creation of numbers and code. It hurt my brain to think about it too much.

I caught in the corner of my eye, Serena smiling at me.

"What?" I asked.

"Nothing," she said. "I'm happy you're here."

I smiled back at her. "I'm happy you're here too."

Shade interrupted our moment by turning around and saying, "You know I have extra powerful hearing, right? You two are so odd. Don't you know the way to show affection is by being enigmatic and hard to read? It makes people love you more."

Serena laughed and I blushed.

The air got hot and humid as we went deeper into the woods. Beads of sweat dampened my cloak. There were less and less trees around us until eventually we arrived at the edge of a murky swamp. A sticky fog hung above the dark green water. Mosquitoes and flies buzzed in the air. This must be the Golpe Swamplands.

A rickety wooden passageway cut across the swamp. I

stepped towards it when Edward held out his hand to stop me. "Wait," he said.

Three shadows grew larger and larger in the water until their long snapping crocodile jaws emerged from the swamp, followed by dark scaled feet. I took in the monsters' stats, thankful for the return of Shade's feline vision ability.

Swamp Croc
Level 12
HP: 390
MP: 11

"It's about time we saw how we fought together," said Edward, unsheathing a glowing metallic sword. "Everyone get ready."

A massive splash came from the swamp as one of the crocs leapt out onto the wet beach. It whipped its tail at us, doing significant damage to Shade and I while pittance to Serena and Edward.

"You two stay back," yelled Serena, gripping her massive sword with two hands. "Let the soldiers handle this."

Shade and I let Edward and Serena take all the aggro of the three crocodile mobs while we stood behind the battle. I gripped my new staff and powered up an energy ball. My staff shook in my hands as it drew upon the surrounding natural mana in the area. Even the energy ball in my hand felt significantly more powerful from the overflow of mana nearby. I whipped it out towards the weakest croc, sending its HP bar to under 15%. Serena came crashing down with her blade, finishing it off.

+105 EXP!

A faint glow of light surrounded Shade as his HP and MP bars replenished. Nice. He must've leveled up. He snuck to the side of the crocodiles, hoping to help out with critical hits.

Serena and Edward each focused on their own croc. It was amazing to watch them fight. So interesting, too, to see two sword wielders fight with such different styles. Edward was all about the long grueling fight. He had the toughness and armor to survive a bloody back and forth. Serena on the other hand was all about dodging, quick steps, and dealing massive amounts of damage in a single blow. After a minute the crocodiles rolled over in defeat.

+105 EXP!
+105 EXP!

Congratulations you have leveled up!
You gain +4 HP
You gain +1 MP
You have (3) unused attribute points that can be applied to any of your five base stats

I grinned at all the prompts stacking in my HUD. I dumped my 3 unused attribute points into spirit, taking my total MP up to 38. With my new apprentice staff my energy balls were dealing a decent amount of damage. Time to focus on being able to summon more of them.

"Congratulations on reaching level 10 Clay," said Serena. "Gaining levels from here on in starts to get quite a bit tougher."

"Aw shit, really?" I said. This wasn't a complete surprise as most games were like this, but I was still disappointed to hear. Leveling up was always a sweet sensation.

"Yeah the game engine sets it up so your experience points stack from level 1 to 10. Meaning you're never too far off between levels. But once you get to level 10, every time you level your total experience points falls back to zero. I think the designers did this as a safety precaution, so new players wouldn't be such vulnerable targets for too long."

"Interesting," I said. "And we're gaining less experience off individual monsters now due to the experience points getting divided across the party." With this knowledge in mind, I'd have to take my 3 additional attribute points much more seriously from now on. I'll only get them in precious segments going forward.

I headed over to the dead swamp crocs and scanned them for loot. Two items came up for each croc.

Slab of Croc Meat (x1)
Croc Scales (x1)

I added the items to my inventory and did the same for the other two croc corpses.

"Ew, what are you doing?" asked Serena.

"Taking loot, what does it look like?"

"What loot? It hasn't dropped any armor or weapons to be sold."

"Yeah but they drop croc meat and scales," I said. "You can use it for crafting."

Both Edward and Serena crossed their arms in disapproval. Classic warrior-types. They were all about the meat and potatoes of the game. I'd played games with similar people. People who'd say, "Crafting is for wimps." I didn't take any of it too much to heart. It meant more loot for me.

"Let's keep moving," said Edward. "Before more crocs come to avenge their fallen brethren."

We headed towards the crooked dock, winding through the swamp. I took a hesitant step to make sure it didn't break and drop me into deadly waters. It was perfectly firm. I stepped onto the dock and we marched down it in a line.

Drooping trees grew out of the small patches in the swamp, hanging over the dock passageway. There was something eerie and strange about this place. A sharp *crack* of twigs rang out. I looked over my shoulder. No one was behind us.

24

We continued down the rickety wooden dock, heading deeper into the middle of the swamp. The air was thick and humid. Bugs buzzed throughout, landing on the back of my neck, forcing me to swat them away. I kept alert, still not completely at ease in this new zone.

"Does anyone else get the feeling we're being watched?"

Shade lifted his finger to his mouth, quieting me down. He nodded his head. His Lirana senses were picking up nearby enemies. But what were they waiting for? Why wouldn't they show themselves?

A snap of wood echoed around us and suddenly my foot shot through the rickety dock and into the water. "Agh. Help!"

Serena grabbed my arm and lifted me up as the hungry jaw of a croc poked out of the swamp water.

"Close call," said Edward. "Let's keep moving. Stay alert."

The shadows of more deadly crocs, slithered beneath the surface of the swamp, intimidating us as we continued further along the docks. We came to a fork in the road, the passage leading in two distinct directions. One headed left, the other to the right.

"Which one should we take?"

"Let's try the left," said Edward. "Any objections?"

Everyone in the party shook their head. His guess was as good as mine.

We moved down the left passage, passing through the mist underneath the shadows of the droopy barren trees. My shoulders twitched, knowing we were being followed. My fingers itched to unsheathe my sword or wield my staff. Why wouldn't these followers show themselves?

Edward stopped moving. The dock stopped in the middle of the swamp. It didn't go any further. It was a dead end.

Uh oh.

This was what our stalkers had been waiting for. Across the swamp, three pairs of bright yellow eyes, poked out of the water. The creatures' heads remained submerged. Only their beady yellow eyes, like periscopes, floated towards us.

Three more sets of eyes came from the other side. One by one, they hopped out of the water and onto the decrepit platform. The bodies beneath the yellow eyes were bright green frog-like creatures. They were shirtless, exposing their smooth green bellies, while they covered up their waists with rags. They held a spear in one hand and a small circular shield in the other. [Golpe Spearman] appeared above their heads.

Golpe Spearman
Level 14
HP: 470
MP: 15

"Looks like we're surrounded," said Shade. "Any ideas knight-man?"

"Stay close," said Edward. "They're trying to intimidate us. They don't wish to fight."

I took a step towards the ones on the dock. "We're not here to hurt you," I said. "We're after a foul creature. Have you seen it?"

The frogs wailed and jabbed their spears in the air, threatening not to come closer.

"Die murderers!" one screamed as it led the charge towards me. Their spears came flying. Serena jumped in front of me, holding her blade horizontally as a shield against the blows.

"Take a step back, Mr. Glass Cannon," said Serena. "Stop trying to take all the hits."

Edward backed into me as the three Golpe spearman from the water jumped onto the other side of the dock, trapping us between them. I was useless here on this dock; more of a hindrance than anything else. I power jumped above the fray to a nearby tree branch to get a better scope of the battlefield.

Serena managed one side while Edward shielded the blows on the other. Shade stayed between the two, jumping into the fray every so often with a quick dagger strike, only to jump back behind the tanks a few seconds later.

I powered up an energy ball and sent it flying towards the group attacking Serena. The Golpe spearman at the rear lifted up his shield in time and blocked the blast. Serena did her jump attack: leaping in the air, both hands wrapped around her giant blade as she smashed it down into the squad of Golpe warriors.

Blocked!

What--? The Golpe wasted no time. Protected behind their wall of shields, they jabbed their spears, taking bit after bit of health off Serena. This shouldn't be happening. Statistically we were much stronger than the Golpe force, even though they did outnumber us. Worse though was they were outmaneuvering us. They were a stronger team than we were. They were working together.

We needed a better plan than our current one and fast.

Edward was shielding all the hits on his end. He buffed himself with a special defense power.

Royal Honour (Buff): *The valor for fighting for what you believe in strengthens and hardens your soul. +5 ATKP +5 TGH (Duration: 3 minutes)*

Even with those benefits, however, he was still battling three trained Golpe spearman all on his own. He kicked one back into the swamp water while the other two quickly came together to create a smaller group shield. We had to get rid of one of their shields to pierce their defenses.

"Shade—steal their shields!"

Shade grinned from across the battlefield. Shade lived to save the day by stealing.

Serena did a massive AOE attack, spinning her blade in a blade tornado. The Golpe spearman weathered the storm as wood chipped from their shields and went flying out into the swamp. I threw another ball down at the defending Golpe as Shade crept forward. He leapt into the fray and quicker than a blink of an eye, leapt back. He held a shield in his hands, grinning.

The Golpe with the missing shield was dumbfounded and confused.

"Now's our chance," I yelled, gripping my staff and

powering up an energy ball. I whipped it down at the defenseless Golpe. The blast ripped into his skin, leaving a burn mark across his shoulder.

-50 HP!

Nice. These creatures' magic defense was clearly not very high. Perfect for me. I rained down energy balls at the Golpe squad. Serena did another leap attack which the warriors blocked. But it didn't matter because now Shade simply jabbed them at their defenseless side. Blood splattered out of their rib cages and showered the swamp. Serena did a side swipe with her blade, slicing off the creatures' eyeballs and sending them flying in the air. Falling towards the water, a croc emerged from the swamp and snatched a pair into its jaws.

There was such a commotion of activity, it was hard to keep track of it all.

With one Golpe squad whittled away, Shade and Serena turned around to assist Edward. I didn't have much MP left so I idled on the tree branch, taking in the battle. If they needed me, I'd jump down and fight with the sword. But, right now strategically, it was better for me to see the whole swamp.

Edward pulled out his shining blade from the Golpe's head, pulling out a burst of blood and flesh with it. He kicked the corpse back into the swamp and wiped the blood off his face.

A list of experience prompts stacked in my HUD.

+123 EXP!
+123 EXP!
+123 EXP!

+123 EXP!
+123 EXP!
+123 EXP!

"Alright—"

A large shadow emerged from the swamp. Ascending from the water was a blue skinned Golpe, riding on top of a massive swamp croc.

Croc Rider
Level 15
HP: 730
MP: 20

"Oh shit," I said. "Guys get back!"

The croc rider galloped across the swamp and leapt onto the docks. Its tail whipped through the air and knocked the party onto their backs, dishing out a whole bunch of damage to all of them.

Edward jumped to his feet and cast Royal Honour on the rest of the party. He lunged his sword forward, stabbing the croc right in its large pink mouth. It snapped shut, mauling at Edward's hands, dealing leaps of damage. Serena swung her sword into the other side of the creature's mouth, forcing him to open it and wail in pain. Edward pulled his sword out and went for another jab. He quickly stabbed it inside the mouth. He yanked his blade out of the creature's tongue, slipping his arm out from the shadows of the creature's jaw.

Thankfully my HP and MP had replenished during the tiny moment of respite between battles, so I powered up an energy ball and whipped it at the rider. The croc tail swung out and blocked the attack, defending the rider.

Interesting. The rider didn't want to get hit. If we took him out, the beast would lose its power.

I unsheathed my sword and power jumped off the tree branch until I hovered over the croc rider. I let myself crash down, sword first. My blade ripped through the Golpe's head, crushing its skull.

Critical Hit!

I crashed onto the croc's scaled back and tried to balance. I pulled my sword out of the Golpe rider, who despite my insane attack, was still conscious and alive. He spun around and came at me with a dagger. I infused my sword with mana, giving it a silvery glow and swung it at the Golpe rider. The magic-infused blade caused the rider to panic and instead of blocking he cowered as the incoming blow sliced his body in half, his intestines spilling onto the scales of the croc.

"Happy you killed the rider," yelled Edward, "But do you mind helping us slay the beast?"

I hurried up along the croc's back to where the rider had been sitting. How had the Golpe kept the beast under its control? I reached out to the loose scales on its back and lifted them up, seeing snot-colored croc skin underneath. As I pulled the scale, the croc screamed in pain, whipping its head erratically.

I scrambled back to my feet, keeping my balance as the croc writhed in all directions. I let my mana course through my arms and into my blade. I lifted the scale and let my silvery sword slip through into the croc's skin. It flipped back and forth and went crazy as a long list of critical hits stacked in my HUD.

The croc rolled into the water, submerging us both

into the swamp. Dirty yellow water surrounded me as the creature thrashed about in the water. I twisted my sword in the creature's weak spot, letting the critical hits stack and stack until finally I got a message for 132 experience points.

The croc's sinking body pulled me with it. I swam out from underneath only to confront a whole group of swamp monsters creeping towards me. *Oh no, oh no, oh no.* I hated any underwater creatures: sharks, piranhas, crocodiles. I needed to get out.

I swam upwards. Hitting the surface, I gasped for air. Both Edward and Serena held their hands out for me to grab. Something clung onto my foot. "C'mon!" I yelled, reaching out for my companion's arms. They yanked me out, saving my legs from being croc dinner.

I collapsed on the dock, heaving with exhaustion. Holy shit. Too scary. Note to self: never power jump onto a croc rider again.

"Good to see you back on the docks," smiled Edward, patting me on the back. "Now you can actually help us out."

The whole group laughed. It was the nervous delirious laugh of people who've stared death way too closely in the eyes.

"Time to get moving," said Serena. "The Golpe weren't attacking us for intruding on their swamp. They think we're murderers."

"Yeah this place is starting to give me the creeps," said Shade, as he bent over and added the Golpe's shields and spears to his inventory.

"Uh guys," I said, pointing out to the swamp. A whole crowd of yellow eyeballs floated across the swamp towards us. At least thirty pairs getting closer and closer.

"We need to run," said Edward.

"Your words, not mine," said Shade, galloping across the docks back the way we came.

My heart pounded as I hurried across the rickety dock. Water splashed as the Golpe leapt out of the swamp and onto the platform. Their webbed feet smacked against the wooden boardwalk. We arrived at the fork in the road and took the other passage.

The war cries of the Golpe echoed behind us. Arrows ripped through the air. I strafed diagonally back and forth as I hurried down the dock. I ran and ran. The mist around me grew thicker and thicker until I ran smack into Shade.

"Um, Shade—I thought we were running for our lives."

"Don't worry," the Lirana said quietly. "They're not going to come here."

Lying in front of us were dozens upon dozens of Golpe corpses, torn apart and left to rot.

25

The stench of dead bodies thickened the air. This was the work of the mutant Skren monster. It tore through hordes of creatures with ease. It was why the Golpe had screamed "murderers" at us when they attacked. They had thought we had reaped this destruction upon them. They were so blinded by hate they never realized we were seeking the same thing: the destruction of this evil creature. What a waste.

Edward and Serena were silent. Each of us dealt with the destruction at our feet in their own way. I took a step onto the island, investigating it. Why were there so many Golpe here in the first place? A line of blood stretched across the ground and led to the mouth of a cave. Except it wasn't exactly a cave: two crumbling columns divided the shrouding mass of darkness. It was the entrance to an underground temple. A dungeon.

"It looks like the creature we seek went down here," said Edward. "Do we follow it into the depths of this ancient crypt?"

The group was battle weary. I wasn't sure if we had it in us.

"Might I add," continued the royal knight. "The monsters down there will be more powerful. It would be wise to go get backup."

"He's right you know," said Serena. "Dungeons are more interactive maps and will spawn mobs based on the level of the adventurers inside. With Edward in our party, it means we will get extra strong mobs."

I considered the small army of Golpe behind us. Going back wasn't right. It only gave the creature down there more time to wreak havoc and destruction in this world. We had to stop it sooner rather than later. It got stronger every minute we wasted.

"I think we should keep going," I said. "We didn't come out here to do a reconnaissance mission. We came to slay the mutation before it gets stronger and ends any more innocent lives."

Serena nodded her head to me, approving my answer. Everyone else did the same.

"Shall we continue?" said Edward.

"Hang on a second," said Shade, toppling over with a pile of spears and shields. They quickly dematerialized into his inventory and he made a face at all of us. "Why are you guys looking at me like that? Loot is loot!"

It was in poor taste, but Shade did have a point. Those spears and shields would net decent coin back in Arondale. I headed over to a nearby body and added a shield and spear to my inventory too. I was left with five slots for whatever other cool stuff we found in the dungeon. Checking out my inventory, though, gave me an idea.

"Hey everyone," I said. "Battling crocs and Golpe is tough. How about a snack?"

I concentrated on my inventory, mixing my apple slices with my honey jar and after mixing the two together, a prompt appeared on my HUD.

You have cooked: Honey Drenched Apple Slices
Ingredients: Apple, Jar of Honey
A perfect afternoon snack. +3% faster HP regeneration while in combat (Duration: 30 minutes)
Your cooking skill increased by 0.3.

I presented the group with my yummy treat. They all came towards me and grabbed a handful. They munched on the snack. In the corner of my vision, the +3% HP regeneration buff flickered beneath their icons.

"And he cooks too," said Serena, flirtatiously.

"Yes," I said, hoping something witty and cool would also follow my initial one-word response but then I remembered I'm Mr. Smooth (aka. an idiot).

I turned to my inventory, pleased I'd now cleared up two more slots, meaning I would be able to loot as hard as Shade. Okay not as intensely as him—I wasn't sure it was possible—but I was happy to have room for more treasure.

Edward and Serena took the first steps into the shadows of the dungeon with Shade and I following behind. It got darker and colder as we descended. I kept my hand against the stone cavernous walls to keep my balance and orient myself while in the murky blackness. We headed downward into the gloom for a good few minutes until a faint glowing light emerged.

At the bottom of the steps was a large cavern lit by a pink radiance coming from the walls. Illuminated crystal shards poked through the stone surrounding the underground cave. Mining picks and wheelbarrows laid about the ground.

"Whoah," I said. "What are these crystals?"

"Crystallized mana," answered Shade.

"It exists underground?"

"Of course it does," he said. "How do you think the continents float in the air like they do?"

I'd never thought about it. Interesting. "But what happens if we mine it all?"

Shade shrugged. "Isn't it obvious?" He then gestured with his hand to mimic a continent falling and crashing into the sea. "But hey, none of the makers of managuns or airships want you thinking about that, so nobody does."

"You better not be making an underhanded comment on the Laergardian Royal Family," said Edward, walking right up to Shade, ready to trade blows.

"Hey guys," I said. "Let's not fight—"

My words get cut off by a rumbling in the ground. The earth at our feet splits open and out comes a horned bug out of the dirt. [Crypt Beetle] hovered above its name as it climbed out onto the cavern's surface. I took in its stats.

Crypt Beetle
Level 20
HP: 1130
MP: 25

Two more beetles climbed out of the hole it dug through and faced us to fight. Edward unsheathed his shining sword and went to work, stabbing the beetle head on. Serena came behind, leaping into the air, and struck down with her massive sword like a butcher cutting through a massive slab of pork. Despite the spectacle of their moves, they didn't deliver much damage.

Staff in one hand, I powered up an energy ball in the other. The power of the ball was more intense than usual. It must've been the staff picking up the excess of mana floating amongst the crystals. I fired it at the beetle Edward was fighting and the damage was so-so. It had equal amounts of magic and normal defense stats.

One beetle did an uppercut attack to Edward in the chest, knocking him back. "They're defense is too high," yelled Serena. "Our attacks aren't doing any damage."

I turned to Shade to see if he had any ideas. But he had completely disappeared.

"Guys—where's Shade?"

The cat thief appeared out of the shadows behind the beetles and lifted one up with his arms. The tiny beetle legs scurried on the ground and dug into Shade, but he simply heaved the beetle until it was upside down, rolling on its curved back.

"Get it while it's down," Shade smiled, pulling out his dagger.

We all attacked the one flipped over beetle, hailing a flurry of attacks at it. Critical hit stacked critical hit until its legs stopped crawling in panic as the life left its body.

+175 EXP!

We turned to the other beetles which were both aggro'd on Edward. His HP was above 50%. He was trading blow for blow with the two beetles. Serena and Shade came up to one and flipped it on its side and went over to the next. As they flipped over the remaining beetle, I pummeled the current upside down one with as many energy balls I had.

Next I ran up to it, infusing my sword with my mana and swiped again and again, slaying the giant insect. When I finished, they had already cleared the other beetle themselves. The stacks rolled by in my HUD.

+175 EXP!
+175 EXP!

Shade glowed as he leveled up again.

I scanned the beetles for items and picked up a beetle horn off each of them. The party was already heading deeper into the cavern by the time I had finished scanning the beetle corpses. I caught up with my team and we continued through the crystalized cavern. The dungeon narrowed and a small archway formed, linking the cavern with another room. We walked through the archway towards the other room with trepidation.

The ground turned from dirt to cobble stone and the room we entered was full of statues. The stone monuments were of old Rorn kings.

"Whose crypt is this?" Serena asked.

Replying to her question, three stone tombs rumbled. The coffin lids slid open and out came ethereal spirits of dead Rorn. They were short and stout like the Rorn, but they lacked a physical nature. They were ethereal, made up of white bluish wisps. One of them wielded a sledge hammer, the other had a battle axe, and the other had a great sword. Their weapons were made of the same ghostly material as they were.

"I do not like the looks of these guys," said Shade.

Rorn Spirit
Level 20

HP: 730
MP: 18

The ghosts ran at us and Serena and Edward met their charge. Steel clashed against the ghost weaponry. I fired up an energy ball and whipped it at the sledgehammer ghost. Shit damage. Damn, high magic defense. Unsurprising: they *were* magical spirits from the afterlife.

I infused my blade and jumped into the battle. My blade swung into the battle-axe spirit, digging into its ghostly flesh. I dug the sword in and out, sawing at its ethereal skin, cutting away health points with every slice back and forth. The spirit decided he'd had enough. Turning his attention away from Serena, he side swiped his battle axe into my stomach. Blood burst from my gut as 30% of my HP fell off. The bleeding debuff flickered onto my status bar.

"Stay out of the way," Edward said, as his blade clashed with the sword-wielding spirit.

"You don't have the toughness to withstand hits from these guys," said Serena. "Stay back."

I stayed back and guzzled down an HP potion. My HP bar restored itself and my disemboweled stomach sealed itself shut, good as new.

Shade circled the battlefield, dancing in and out of the fray. He front-flipped into striking distance and threw out a nasty backstab with his dagger and then back flipped out to safety.

Serena unleashed a blade tornado, twirling between the three spirits, ricocheting between them like a deadly pinball until their red HP bars fell to zero. They exploded into dust, littering the cracks of the stone floor.

+175 EXP!

+175 EXP!
+175 EXP!

I walked over to the fallen blue dust on the ground and it registered in my HUD as "Spirit Dust." I picked it up and added it to my inventory. Crafting materials for the win.

The bricks of the center wall moved and rolled back, forming a secret archway. The killing of those three spirits had triggered the opening of another room. When the door fully emerged, a purple shadow swirled in front of it.

"Looks like we found the end of the dungeon," said Serena. "The purple shadow signals the room inside is a boss room. If we run through the shadow, we can't come back until the boss is defeated or—" Serena didn't finish her sentence.

"The mutant skren bandit must've gone in there," I said.

I turned to Shade and Edward. "Are you guys sure you want to go in there? If Serena and I go in—we'll come back even if we die. It's not the same for you."

"A royal knight never leaves his party behind," said Edward. "If you two are going to fight whatever lies beyond this shadow, then I'll join you."

"And Shade?"

The cat thief smiled and said, "You think I'd run away now? After fighting Skren, Golpe, giant beetles, and Rorn spirits. I'm sorry mate, but I've already been given plenty of excuses to leave. Yet here I am. Also, lest we all forget, rare creatures mean rare loot."

"Okay then," I said. "It's settled."

I took a step forward when Serena put her hand on my arm.

"Clay," she said. "Can I talk to you over here a minute?"

We stepped off to the side and Serena's face was

intensely serious. "Clay—we can't enter the room thinking we'll be okay if we die. Those players I saw fighting a similar monster never came back. You've already been branded by it in your death. If it kills us, it's forever. Are you still sure we should go in there?"

I gulped. The harsh reality wasn't pretty. But we hadn't come all this way only to decide now the mission was too dangerous.

"Whatever happens, we have each other's back, right?"

Serena smiled, "Of course. You're my spell caster, my DPS."

"And you're my tank," I replied.

I walked back to the group. I pulled my staff from behind my shoulder and gripped it in my hand. "No more wasting time," I said, charging through the shadow gate. "Let's fight this thing."

The boss arena was a massive square chamber with high ceilings. Dungeon moss and vines grew around the stone columns in each corner of the room. It reeked of death and decay. Off to the side, lying in a pool of blood, was a dead creature.

I walked towards it.

"Clay," Serena said. "Watch out. We don't know if this room is trapped."

Heeding my friend's advice, I took each step carefully as I moved towards the dead creature. Crimson scars ran across the different amputated pieces of the body. When I finally stood over top of its deformed snout, drenched in a puddle of blood, there was no denying it. This dead thing in front of me was the mutant Skren bandit.

Did it come to this place to die? Or did something more powerful kill it?

The floor at my feet trembled. The walls rumbled. Appearing in the center of the room was a ball of wispy light. The ball grew and grew until—_pop_—a gigantic specter of a Rorn king appeared. He was like spirits in the other room but ten times the size. His knees were at our eye level. The sheer power and energy coursing through him blasted his silver hair above his head.

This was the boss of the dungeon. Or, at least, it had been. The spirit wasn't completely ethereal. Stretching from his right shoulder where a wispy blue spirit arm should've been was an enlarged Skren arm with claws. What the--? The mutant Skren and the Rorn spirit had combined into this ultimate horrific creature.

The boss was duel-wielding. He had a silver spectral battle axe in one hand and in the other was the Skren arm, black worms festering off the fur. The mutant arm which had instant killed me with a single touch last time. I shuddered.

The mutant Rorn spirit turned to us, its fragmented caption popping up above its head: [Rorn SP3r1t K3ng]. I pulled up its stats.

Rorn SP3r1t K3ng
Level: ??
HP: ??
MP: ??

"Well's let's not stand here," yelled Serena, running forward, dragging her giant blade with both her hands behind her.

"Agreed," said Edward, running towards the spirit, sword in hand.

"I'll see what I can do from behind," said Shade, sneaking towards the walls and heading around the boss.

I gripped my staff and powered up an energy ball, throwing it at the huge spirit in front of me. It did damage but not much. What was I going to do? How was I going to help here? I had to figure out how to beat this thing. Where was its weak spot?

Serena and Edward went back and forth landing blows on the side of the spirit. But the ghost of the Rorn king had had enough. He gripped his axe with both hands and did a wide radius swipe across the room. Both Edward and Serena fell back, roughly 40% of their HP being knocked off in a single blow.

Holy shit. This creature was strong. 40% HP off Serena and Edward—such an attack would've instant killed me for sure. It was a good thing I was firing support blasts from the back then.

Edward and Serena each guzzled down an HP potion and Edward recast the Royal Honor buff on both of them. In seconds they were back to swinging against the monster. They circled around it as they fought. The giant spirit turned on its feet, struggling to keep up with them. He swiped his Skren arm but they were always a few meters away from where he targeted.

Leaping out of the shadows, Shade appeared with his dagger in hand. He landed a critical hit in the back and dragged the blade through the wispy spirit flesh. The boss cried out in pain. It quickly turned away from Serena and Edward and swiped its claw out towards Shade. The thief jumped away and fell on his back.

Oh no. Shade was wearing light armor like me. One hit and he'd be a goner and there was no coming back for Shade.

I summoned a large energy ball and whipped it at the spirit's back. Please draw aggro to me. The attack landed but it did no use in changing the boss's target. The spirit's hate was fully on Shade now.

Shade crawled backwards to escape the monster's

shadow. It lifted its Skren arm, readying its instant kill attack. Right as it was about to thrust its arm right through Shade's chest, Serena leapt in the air and stabbed the Skren arm, forcing the spirit boss to recoil in pain and confusion. It turned around, all of its aggro back on Serena and Edward.

Phew. Too close.

The boss's HP bar, despite being undefined in the stats, was around the 55% mark. We were slowly whittling it away. Victory was in our sights. Edward and Serena chipped away at the boss's health until the bar dropped to 50%.

The boss lifted both its hands in the air and channeled power for an AOE attack. The rocks from the ceiling fell. Small ones and large ones. There was no safe place to hide from the incoming onslaught. It would kill us all.

"Come to me," yelled Edward, lifting his shining blade in the air. A liquid orb enveloped Edward and the area around him. I dashed across the ruptured ground and leaped into the protective bubble. Shade jumped in from the other side. Rocks crashed all around us but none broke through Edward's magic force field.

The rocks stopped falling and the spirit returned to normal fighting mode.

"I won't be able to protect us like that again," said Edward. The re-cast time on the spell must be super slow. "We need to give it everything we got before it unleashes the attack again."

Edward and Serena returned to hitting the mutated ghost king with their blades. I power up another energy ball and knock it in the chest. We were fighting on a timer now. We needed to destroy it before it did the earthquake move again.

Where was its weak spot? Back in my first fight with the

Skren bandit, the best attack I had landed was in its eye. But the spirit was ten times my height. So? I was a fucking power jumping Aeri.

I ran full speed towards the spirit boss. I leapt into the air, created a mana platform and jumped again. I did this a few times until I hovered way above Serena and Edward, flying full speed towards the Rorn king's head. I unsheathed my sword, infusing it with mana as I did so, and did one final power jump, propelling myself right at the spirit's head, particularly its ghostly eyeball. My sword blasted through the spirit's pupil. I worried the attack would fly through the spirit, but when my sword landed it physically puncture the ghost flesh. A white gravelly dust spurted forth from its eye as I stabbed it over and over. I slid onto the spirit's shoulder and kept swinging my mana infused sword all over its face and neck.

The spirit boss flailed its arms.

"Get the hell outta there Clay," yelled Serena. "You can't handle all the aggro. It will kill you!"

"Don't worry about me," I yelled. "Let's finish this."

I kept stabbing the creature in the head, over and over. While the rest of the party did damage down below. The creature kept moving so erratically, I'd occasionally fall off the ghostly shoulder, but I would power jump back on. With me hitting it in its critical zone, it wasn't able to reorient itself or deal direct damage to anyone else. We all stabbed our sharp weapons in and out of its spirit skin. Again and again. Its HP bar slowly decreased. It went down to 5%... 4%... 3%...2%...1%.

"C'mon," I yelled, ripping my sword free and lunged it back into the creature's eye.

I waited for the experience bonus to flash across my

HUD. But nothing happened. The creature was still alive. I stabbed it again. Then another time.

"It's not taking damage," yelled Serena from below.

What? It only had 1% of health left. There must be something missing here.

The boss spun and I fell off of it. I power jumped at the last minute to cushion my landing to the floor.

The spirit lifted both its hands up towards the ceiling. Oh no. The AOE attack. We won't be able to defend against it. Unbelievable. After all of this, we had lost. Serena and Edward desperately sliced their swords into the spirit's legs, hoping to land a final killing blow. But it wasn't happening.

This was it. We were all going to die. I had failed. I didn't have the strength to save my friends. I had been given a second chance and yet again, I had failed to be the person I wanted to be. I was a failure, just as my mother and father had always thought.

Rocks fell from the ceiling. First small ones but the big body crushing ones would come soon.

A burning sensation enveloped my wrist. What was happening? I didn't see any of my HP drain. I pulled off my gloves and saw the black swirl on my wrist had spread and was enveloping my arm and turning my veins black.

What was happening to me?

My arm jerked forward and an intense energy swarmed through my wrist and blasted out of my hand.

Everything went black.

27

//run: virus_scan
//run: fragmentation
//run: defragmentation
//run: restore_corrupted_file
//run: VRmodelling_render
//run: destroy_file

I fell through a sea of numbers and code. I didn't know how long I'd been falling for. I couldn't move, I could only descend. What was happening to me?

The girl from my dreams flickered in front of me.

"Why are you hurting me?" she screamed.

"I don't know what's happening," I said.

The girl was crying.

"Why are you doing this to me? Leave me alone!"

Darkness enveloped me.

*** _RunComplete00 ***

I GASPED AWAKE, my arms clawing into the air, grasping at the space above, hoping to grab onto something real. Serena's head appeared in my vision, her chest and body looming over me. She smiled and said, "Guys! He's alive."

She fell on me, hugging me with all her strength. She gave me a kiss on the cheek and whispered, "I'm so happy you survived."

I hugged her back, squeezing her chest into mine, as the sky above shone down on us. Sunlight leaked through a massive hole in the corner of the ceiling.

Quest Failed: Mystery Creature in the Woods

"The monster," I said. "Did it escape?"

Serena nodded her head and opened her mouth to say something, when Edward Silver pounced on me. He grabbed me by my coat's collar and shook me.

"You never told me you dabbled in forbidden magic," he yelled, face reddening. "You're no worse than the thing we were fighting. I can't believe I ever fought alongside someone like you."

You have lost status with Edward Silver, Captain of the Royal Knights of Laergard, Arondale Outpost (Eastern Laergard). You have fallen from neutral alignment to "distrusted" status.

Warning: If you descend into further negative alignment, such as "outcast" status, you will no longer be able to enter towns or cities with Royal Knight outposts.

He threw me back against the floor and walked out of the dungeon. His face and stats in my party menu disappeared. The black mark on my wrist burned. Eve, the innkeeper, had warned me this mark would get me into trouble. I didn't realize it would hold such social stigma.

Shade handed out his furry hand to me and said, "Don't worry about him. Typical Royal Knight behavior. Always so stiff and law abiding." He yawned. "No fun whatsoever."

I grabbed Shade's hand and he lifted me off the ground. "Tell me what happened after I fell unconscious."

"A giant blast came out of your palm—like a laser beam —except it was pitch black," said Serena. "Your blast hit the creature in the shoulder and it screamed out, wailing—"

The little girl's voice shot through my memory: *Why are you hurting me?*

"And then it leapt in the air, punched a hole through the cavern's wall and escaped."

"Thank goodness too," added Shade. "We were all seconds way from being crushed by the beast's earthquake spell."

"There's something about the mutated creature we don't fully understand," I said. "I don't know if we're going about it the right way. Is killing it really the answer?"

"We're not strong enough to kill it right now even if we wanted to," Serena said. "Let's get out of here."

The three of us headed back through the dungeon. It was pretty easy as no new mobs had respawned. But it was depressing as we hadn't beaten the boss. We had travelled all the way to the bottom only to fail. What a waste of our time. The horrible mutated amalgam was still out there. Still roaming the land, threatening everything in its path.

The Golpe swamplands was empty when we got out of the cave. I turned to Serena, "Should we fast travel to Arondale?"

Serena shook her head. "Let's hold off. Shade won't be able to."

It was crazy the privileges players had over NPCs. Did the NPCs resent human players for this fact?

We trudged through the forest until eventually we entered the farmland meadow

on the outskirts of Arondale.

"Well that adventure yielded a much less substantial amount of loot than I'd been hoping for," said Shade. "This calls for only one thing: ale! I'll be at the Crow's Heart if you need me."

Shade's party icon flickered away as he ran off towards the city.

Serena stared off into the sunset.

"What now? Our current party is too small to go after the mutation." I scratched the back of my head. "I know this sounds ridiculous but did you wanna take a break? See if the market is still open? I saw really tasty treats I wanted to try."

Serena shook her head and she wiped something from her eye.

"What's wrong?"

"I'm fine," said Serena, sounding totally not fine. "The market sounds nice, but I don't know if I can do it tonight. I'm going to fast travel to Land's Shield and go to the library there. As with today's quest, clearly the game's algorithms and A.I. are incorporating game mechanics—quests and the like—to deal and control the problem; there must be more information hidden in the history and lore of the world."

"Do you really have to do that tonight?" I asked, regretting it as soon as I said it.

Serena nodded. "Meanwhile, you need to complete your class quest. And—" She held back a sob. "Survive the night."

I had briefly forgotten my time here in Illyria was potentially almost over. This was why she was acting so weird.

"Even with our failed quest, it's been the best afternoon I've had in A.K.O. so far. But I don't know what I'll do if I don't hear from you tomorrow. That's why we can't see each other until then. Thinking about it right now is already destroying me on the inside. So good luck Clay and hopefully see you soon. I'll need your help destroying the mutation."

She came towards me and leaned her head into mine and we kissed. I reached up to touch her but my hand merely swiped through her vanishing body. She was fast travelling away, the tears in her eyes disintegrating into pixelated dust and then nothing at all.

28

I stood on the hill as the windmills spun below me. Farmers returned from their hard day in the fields to their homes for supper while I stayed frozen on the hill above. I didn't budge an inch, lingering in the spot where Serena and I had just been together. I still felt her lips touching mine. I didn't want to let go of the moment.

When I dropped out of university I didn't want to see anyone. I didn't want to confront any of my classmates. Their judgment would have been too much. I wanted to escape. I withdrew my college fund without talking to my parents and booked a plane ticket to Europe. I didn't say goodbye to anyone. After all those years, I only regretted not saying goodbye to one person. Not my father. Not my mother or brother. No. The only person I wished I'd seen before I left was Serena. For years, I accepted I'd never see her again. Now through a demented turn of fate, we were both cursed with the ZERO virus and wound up in this strange fantasy purgatory. My second chance with her existed beyond the slow dipping sun, in the world of tomorrow. The kiss felt more real than I'd ever imagined kissing her would be like. My eyes welled up, knowing this second chance—with Serana but also at life—was far from guaranteed.

The swoosh of an airship flying overhead snapped me out of my melancholic daze. I shook my head. Wallow time was over. There was still daylight left. If this were potentially my last day alive in here, well I'd make the most of it. With a new found determination, I moved down the hill towards Arondale.

The city was quieter than it had been earlier in the day. Less adventurers roamed the streets—they were still out grinding in the forest and fields or locked into a longer quest chain. Merchants were deconstructing their market stalls and packing their leftover wares into caravans. One food stall was still open, the whiff of its savory delicious smell leading me to it. A Muumuu couple was serving bear meat sandwiches with melted cheese and mustard. It was ten gold coins for one. I handed the money to the woman and the man handed me the sandwich wrapped in a napkin.

I took a bite and the salty flavor of the sandwich burst in my mouth. The rough texture of the meat mixed perfectly with the mustard and cheese. I took another bite and then another until before I knew it I had gobbled the whole thing and had nothing but residual crumbs on my fingers.

Well-Fed (Buff): You gain 3% faster HP and MP regeneration (Duration: 20 minutes)

Great. Not only did I feel way better with food in my stomach, I was being rewarded for it too. With food in my belly, I headed over to Frederik's shop. He was about to close but I asked if he wanted to buy any loot off me. I sold him my rough leather boots, the Golpe spear and shield for twenty-five gold coins.

I wished him a pleasant evening and continued on my way. It wasn't dark yet and I had one last thing I wanted to accomplish today. I headed through the quiet streets of Arondale to the west gate. I hurried through the meadow, ignoring the bumblebee and mosquito prey, and through the apple orchard to the tall windmill on the hill. I knocked on the door. It swung open and there stood Theobold, red in the face from another interruption, grumpy as ever.

"Isn't it late for questing?"

"You told me to come back when I'd learned my innate skills. Well, I have."

Theobold crossed his arms and grunted. "Oh really? Care to prove it to me?"

I didn't waste any time. I took a step back from the door and let the mana inside of me run to the tips of my fingers and emerge in a glowing orb of light.

"The energy ball, yes," said Theobold. "You showed me this morning."

I jumped in the air and created platforms of mana at my feet, allowing me to jump higher and higher. Up in the air, I let myself fall, occasionally creating a small platform to steady myself back to the ground.

Not one to mince words, Theobold grunted in approval.

Finally, I unsheathed my sword and held it above my head. Once again I let the mana inside me course through to my fingertips where I gently let it envelop the blade of my sword in a shining silver glow. I did this for a few seconds and then brought the sword back down and sheathed it at my side.

I turned to Theobold to see what he thought.

The old Rorn mage scratched his chin and said, "Good. Now the real trial can begin."

29

Real trial!?

"But I thought learning those abilities was the trial," I whined.

Theobold shook his head. "Are you kidding? There are Aeri children who can do all those things and we don't grant them the powers of a mage, now do we?"

The old man stepped outside and slammed the door shut. "Come with me."

I followed him behind the windmill. He stepped inside the carriage of his hot air balloon. "Get in," he said.

While I generally believed it was a good idea not to get into hot air balloons with strange older men, I would have to make an exception. He removed the powerful staff from his back and raised it in the air, summoning fire and air into the balloon, lifting us above his windmill and into the clouds.

The meadow and apple orchard below us were now nothing but tiny specks.

"This is incredible," I said. "And you're operating it with magic?"

Theobold grunted as he continued to manipulate the elements around him and navigate his balloon ship deeper and deeper into the clouds.

"You're doing it all without mana crystals as well," I exclaimed.

"Hrmph. So you've learnt a bit about this world then, huh?"

The way he phrased the question was odd but I wasn't sure why.

"Yes. There are indeed alternative forms of sky travel than the airship. But the economy of the mana crystals is what dominates the political machinations of Illyria. A peaceful, less harmful solution to all the continents problems is not in the interest of the various ruling classes."

The rants and ravings of a curmudgeonly old man faded in the background as I day dreamed of manipulating fire and operating my own type of airship: be it a hot air balloon or something else. Taking to the skies was thrilling.

We travelled through a wet mist of vapor until we arrived in a small cavernous passageway of clouds. The sun poked through like an eye peering through a keyhole. At the top floated a small floating island, no bigger than a large slab of rock. Theobold lifted his staff and made different actions with his fingers, manipulating the elements so we landed the balloon ship on the small island.

The floating slab of rock housed two stone columns, between which glowed a purple swirling portal.

"You must pass through there," said Theobold, stepping out of the balloon carriage. "To attempt the trial of the mage. If you succeed, you gain the apprentice mage class."

"And if I fail?"

"The class is closed for you forever."

I gulped. My build wouldn't suit many other classes. I'd already dumped my stats in the appropriate base stats. Shit. If this didn't work out I would be seriously disadvantaged for the rest of my time here in A.K.O. Whatever class I'd potentially do instead, my stats would be sub-optimal to everyone else who knew what they were doing. I'd be less welcome in parties and guilds. Life would simply be more tough for me than it already was.

Fuck that.

"When you enter the trial," said Theobold. "You'll be temporarily given the apprentice mage class kit to use. Take a moment to study it before you continue on."

I nodded my head and walked to the portal. It was time to become a mage.

I STEPPED through the portal and found myself in a temple built of stone. A large staircase stood in front of me. I wasn't sure where it led; I was unable to see the top. Windows scattered across the stone walls let through rays of light and showed off the bright blue sky and clouds of the world outside.

An immense pain rushed through my head. I collapsed to the ground. It was like the worst migraine or headache I'd ever felt. I gripped my head, massaging my scalp from the intense throbbing. Tears leaked out of my eyes. What was happening to me? Then, as quickly as the pain had arrived, it disappeared. A prompt appeared in my HUD:

Temporary Class Unlocked: Apprentice Mage

As a student of mana, you harness the raw energy of the world around you, taking control of the four elements to unleash your power.

Effect 1: +5% faster MP regeneration
Effect 2: +25 Spirit
Effect 3: +25 MTKP
Effect 4: +10% resistance from mana-based attacks
Effect 5: Access to Apprentice Mage restricted abilities
Effect 6: Cannot wear heavy armor
Effect 7: Cannot wield heavy weapons

Whoah. The pain I must've experienced must've been my brain downloading all of the class's knowledge and insights. I clicked on the new abilities prompt and more windows appeared.

Temporary New Abilities Unlocked: *You feel a heightened sense of the elements around you—such is the way when studying the power of mana. Spend Class Skill Points to unlock new abilities on your class skill tree. You gain 1 Class Skill Point every time you level up. You can also level up your abilities by using them frequently.*

I checked the amount of Class Skill Points I currently possessed. I had gained the amount I would have had if I had gained this class at level one, so I had ten points to spend.

Starting abilities:

Fire: Fire is every mage's weapon of choice. Fire abilities deal direct damage to your opponents.

Fire Blast: Shoot an orb of molten lava at your enemies
MTKP: 30-50
MP Cost: 8

Water: Water provides life to all living things. Water abilities heal and strengthen you and your party members.

Healing Mist: Create an enchanted mist around you
Ability: Heal 60 HP
MP Cost: 8

Air: Air is all around us, manipulating all of our movements. Air abilities control and debuff your enemies.

Lightning Cage: Paralyze an opponent with a cage made of lighting.
Ability: Opponent is paralyzed for 10-15 seconds
MP Cost: 10

Earth: Harnessing the Earth means manipulating the very ground at your feet. Earth abilities deal damage to a wide area of enemies.

Earthquake: Make the ground around you tremble and erupt with jagged rocks
MTKP: 25-100 (5 meter radius)
MP: 20

Amazing. I'd taken ages to get three abilities and now in a single stroke I'd gained four more. Each element had its own skill tree, unlocking more abilities when I spent skill points there. It was possible to spend points on current abilities, strengthening skills I was already comfortable with. The tables and systems were immense. I'd have to sit down for days to study what kind of mage I'd want to be. I had so many options. I gave a cursory glance at the higher-level abilities and some of it was absolutely insane. Fire had an ability called supernova. It created a massive meteor in the sky to pummel your opponent with. Earth had an ability to summon an Earth golem—which would be extremely useful for solo play as it would tank for me.

A giant grin formed on my face. But I was getting ahead of myself. I still needed to test out my current abilities. I opened the palm of my hands and thought *fireball*. A ball of flame ignited in my hand. Somehow my mind intuitively knew how to summon a fireball now. I threw the ball at the nearby wall. It blasted and dissipated in a shower of smoke and ash.

Okay, let's try the water skill. *Healing mist*. Somehow it was less intuitive than the fireball spell. I already had known how to do energy ball but how did you summon healing mist? When I stopped overthinking it, my shoulders stretched back and locked into place. I lifted my head and a moist wafting mist surrounded me, comforting my skin.

The lightning spell came easy like the fireball. An intense crackle of lighting emerged from my hands. It transformed into a cage and shot forth. Had an enemy been present, the cage would've locked it into place. Instead it crashed into the wall with a crackle and snap.

The ground rumbled. Something was coming. At the top of the stairs, a spider the size of a small child appeared. Except it wasn't a normal spider. It was made of metal and silver and bright energy glowed out from the center of it. It was an artificial spider creation. It crawled down the steps. Easy peasy. Especially with my new abilities.

But then another spider appeared and then another until the whole staircase was a mass of metal spiders coming to attack me.

30

The spiders descended the stairs. I summoned a fireball and whipped it at one. The mechanical insect crackled in destruction. I formed another one and shot it out again. There were too many of them though for individual fireballs. I needed an AOE attack. Good thing I was about to test one out.

I ran up the stairs stepping over the jagged metal spider legs, surrounding myself by the treacherous creatures. Their claws dug into my legs causing me immense pain, but I ignored it. I thought to myself *earthquake* and my arms knew to stretch out and grip the air at the sides and pull upward as if dragging the ground beneath by a thick rope. The floor at my feet trembled, the floor ruptured and stones floated above me. The spiders at my feet all tripped over themselves and crackled as they lost their sense of gravity. All of the lights glowing from their centers faded away.

Nice. *Earthquake* was a sweet as fuck spell. I kicked the metal spiders as I hurried up the stairs. First part of the trial: *completed*. The trial must be all about testing my abilities with the different elements.

At the top of the stairs was a long stone foyer leading to a door. Easy. But when I got to the door it wouldn't budge. I summoned a fireball and blasted it which did nothing. Brute strength wasn't the way to go here. I noticed a small keyhole. But where was the key?

I peered at the mound of dead robot spiders littering the stairs. Did one of them hold the key as loot? I stepped down the staircase. Something giggled behind me. I spun around. A metal pixie floated in the air, its tiny hands clutching onto an old skeleton key.

"Hey, give that to me," I said, snatching in the air, but the pixie flew out of reach.

Time for air magic. My hands crackled as I threw out my lightning cage spell, sending out a cube of electricity at the floating pixie, trapping it in my lightning cage. I pulled my hand back and the cage floated back to me. I summoned a fireball in my hand, intimidating the winged creature with my power.

"Give me the key or become barbequed pixie—your choice."

The pixie lifted up the stone key to me and I snatched it out of its hands.

"Good decision," I said. I went and put the key in the lock and twisted the door open.

A dim innocuous passageway stood in front of me. I took a step inside and felt a searing pain come from all directions. The hallway drained my health, my HP bar plummeting. I quickly retreated back to the entrance. Holy crap. How was I supposed to get through there? As I let my HP replenish back to full, I understood what I had to do. I stepped back inside the passage. The intense pain returned but I wasn't nervous about it. I cast healing mist and felt my body relax, my HP bar replenish. The spell lasted about three seconds and then the pain came back. I kept moving through the hall, casting healing mist, to counteract the damage of the hallway's painful air. I pushed through the passage, trudging forward as my HP boomeranged up and down.

Eventually I made it to the end, gasping for air as I took in the next room, a darkened chamber. Four pillars made up a platform where a fifth pillar stood, glowing a white light.

What was I supposed to do in here?

I cast fireball to illuminate the room, revealing unlit torches on the pillars. I went towards them, lighting them with fireball. When I lit the fourth and final pillar, the whole room came alight. Torches all throughout the ceiling lit up.

The white pillar in the middle glowed and out of nowhere a ghostly spirit appeared overtop. He was disembodied, only the upper half of his body floated in the air. His face and body was concealed by cloak. *Uh oh*. Would I have to fight this thing?

"Congratulations young pupil," spoke the mystical being. "You have passed the trials of the apprentice mage. You now face a challenging choice. You must choose the element you find yourself most aligned with. Which one spoke to you the most? Choose wisely."

Interesting. I guess I had to decide whether I wanted to be a fire mage or water mage or whatever else. I didn't know which spells I liked the most though. I liked the Earth AOE but I enjoyed the control spells of air. The water healing spell was extremely useful and while I already had energy ball, fire ball was ten times cooler.

I didn't know which one to choose. Every time I came to a decision, I would remember something else. I was about to pick Earth but then I recalled Theobold operating his balloon ship with wind magic. Did I really want to pass such an ability up?

Shit. This was a hard decision.

But hang on. This was a major game decision and it hadn't appeared as a prompt in my HUD. I guess not every decision would, but this felt like the sort of thing where you'd get consulted with tables and charts. What if this wasn't an actual decision but a test in and of itself?

"Every element compliments the other," I said. "You can't have one without the others. It's foolish to choose one."

The ghost mage nodded his head. "So you'll forego even having mastery over one of them if you cannot have all? Is this your final answer?"

I wasn't sure if the ghost was hinting at me to change my answer, but I stayed determined in my choice. "Yes."

A withered smile appeared beneath the hood of the ghost mage. "A wise answer indeed. Clay Hopewell you have shown both true aptitude for magic and a wisdom to wield it responsibly. You are hereby granted the class: Apprentice Mage!"

A pop-up window appeared in my vision.

Class Unlocked: *Apprentice Mage!*

Hell yeah!

31

The ghost mage flickered away, revealing behind him a swirling portal. I stepped through and emerged back below the clouds in front of Theobold's windmill home. The old Rorn mage was sweeping the ground in front of his doorway.

"So, you passed the trial, eh?"

The man kept his back to me as he said it. He stopped sweeping, leaving his broom against the wall of the house and went inside. He came back with a cool navy blue coat.

"Why don't you throw this on, start looking like a real mage."

I took the cloak in my hands and a prompt appeared in my HUD.

New Item Alert! Basic Mage Coat (DEF: 15. +10 MTKP. Durability 7/10)
Do you wish to equip (Yes/No)?

I equipped the coat and felt more powerful as I dawned it. I wanted to message Serena right then about completing the apprentice mage trials. But I'd hold off. She said she didn't want to hear from me until tomorrow.

Arondale glittered in the setting sun. Rays reflecting off the glass of the aerodome and the church roof. But something wasn't right. A cloud of black smoke billowed out from the city center. I took a few steps, wincing. What was happening down there?

A shadow of a giant creature loomed over Theobold and I. Spinning around, a magnificent yellow gryphon flapped its wings as it lowered itself to the ground. Riding the giant bird was none other than Kendara.

"Theobold—the Eldra Aeri of Forbidden Forest need your help." She turned to me next. "We can use your assistance as well Clay. Something attacked one of the mother raptors in our forest, sending it into a monstrous rage. We don't know what happened to it exactly. But it's since escaped our rangers and is attacking the township of Arondale. Only you can help us stop it."

A quest prompt appeared in my HUD.

New Quest Alert: Save Arondale!

Arondale is under attack from a deadly creature. If it isn't stopped (in 29:58 minutes) it will destroy parts of Arondale forever.
Quest Type: Unique
Quest Difficulty: Hard
Reward: 3000 EXP
Accept: Yes/No ?

It wasn't a hard to decision in the least. I accepted the quest straightaway. I needed to help Arondale. No question. Another figure appeared in the distance, running across the apple orchard towards us. It was Shade.

"Clay—Arondale's in trouble. Another one of those mutant things is attacking the town!"

Theobold interjected. "What are these mutant things?"

"Demons, foul creatures," Shade explained. "They take over creatures right as they're about to die and possess them from the inside."

"Sounds like what happened to the mother raptor," said Kendara.

Theobold's eyes widened. Had he seen such horrors before?

"We must go to town at once," he said. "Hurry. Let's party up."

Theobold Longstaff would like to join your party! Accept (Yes/No)?

I accepted the old mage and was overwhelmed when I saw his stats.

Theobold Longstaff
Level: 99
Race: Rorn
Class: Wizard of the Light

HP: 601
MP: 265

ATKP: 26
MTKP: 160
TGH: 26
SPIRIT: 161
LUCK: 24

Level 99—are you serious? The highest level in the game. I expected Theobold to be quite a high level but not the highest level possible. The old Rorn smirked at me.

Shade joined the party next along with Kendara. I sent a quick message via the HUD to Serena. I knew she'd want to be here to help us defeat this thing. We didn't have time to wait for her. But if she got the message in time she would be able to fast travel and help us out.

The plume of black smoke got bigger and bigger around Arondale. Holy shit. Are we even ready to take this thing on? We still didn't know how to defeat it. Was my new class and abilities going to be enough?

"There's no time to waste," yelled Kendara, hopping onto her mount. "Clay get on."

I ran towards her gryphon. Kendara held out her hands to me and lifted me up onto the large bird.

"Wrap your hands around my waist," she said.

I felt awkward but I knew there was no time for horny boy bullshit at the moment, so I did as I was told. I clasped my hands together around her waist.

The Aeri gripped her hands and massaged the neck of the gryphon. She bent over and whispered in its ear. "Fly us to Arondale so we can stop the mother raptor."

The gryphon flapped its wings and we slowly took off into the air. The wind blew our hair back as we soared through the sky. We flew far above the apple orchard and beginner training zone with Arondale in our sights.

"Don't forget us," yelled Shade.

I turned around and saw Shade and Theobold were together in the hot air balloon. The old Rorn mage was casting wind spells, manipulating the currents of the air to propel their ship forward, sweeping through the sky right behind us.

The tall magnificent buildings of Arondale came into view as we flew right over the walls. Erupting like a black hole at the center of the town was a gigantic tyrannosaurus-rex. Godzilla sized. But like the Skren Bandit Leader and the Rorn Spirit Lord before it, this dinosaur was a bizarre amalgamation of all the creatures it had absorbed in its corruptive glitch-fueled state. Half of its rib cage had the blue spectral dust of the Rorn Spirit lord and where one of its raptor arms should be was a limply hanging Skren arm—grown to dinosaur scale —with black worms coursing through its patchy skin.

We flew through the clouds of smoke, moving closer and closer to the deadly creature. Kendara pulled the gryphon skyward to avoid being hit by the barrage of mana bullets being shot from below at the demonic dinosaur.

Next she swung down through the clouds directly at it. My stomach dropped as we got closer. Its head was ten times the size of Kendara and I, even including the gryphon. The creature's caption popped into view above its forehead: [Gr8 Moth3r R^ptor]. It stretched out its neck and opened its jaw to chomp us to bits. We were no longer fully in the air but rather in the shadows of the creature's giant mouth. We zoomed through, passing the clutches of its pincer teeth, escaping their sharp sting.

"Do you plan on attacking or will I have to fly my gryphon and fight this creature as well?

I let go of my arms from Kendara's waist and balanced myself. The gryphon swerved in the air, back in the direction of the giant t-rex. I powered up a fireball in my hands and shot at the creature's head. HP knocked off it but the dino wasn't bothered.

In the distance, on the side of the dinosaur's snout was Shade and Theobold, strafing through the air in the hot air balloon. Shade was holding a mana pistol and was firing relentlessly. Theobold gripped his staff and waved his arms summoning a massive meteor from the sky which came crashing down like a galactic right hook into the creature's face. Of course—Theobold had the supernova ability. And I bet it was one of his weaker moves.

I whipped another fireball at the creature's eyeball, doing another pittance of damage. Kendara kept the gryphon swerving from one side of the dinosaur's jaws to the other, keeping its head chasing after us. I threw another blast at it.

Despite all the damage raining down on the creature, its HP was hardly diminishing at all. It was resting comfortably at 80% of its HP and we had hit the twenty minute mark in the duration of our quest.

We needed to hit it with more than pure strength and damage. We needed critical hits. We needed to find its weak spot.

I had an idea.

"Kendara," I said. "This sounds crazy but can you get us caught between its teeth again."

"Are you crazy?"

"Trust me. I have an idea."

Kendara shook her head and grinned at the madness of what she was about to do. She gripped the fur of the gryphon and angled him back towards the demonic dinosaur. We zoomed through the air directly towards the monster. It opened its jaws and wailed at us, baring the deep insides of its throat. Our final resting place if my plan didn't work.

"Keep going," I said.

We were right in the dino's mouth. The teeth were

closing in on us and all it would have to do was swallow and down we'd go.

I lifted both my arms and summoned earthquake from within the dino's jaws. The whole inside of its mouth vibrated. Its teeth rattled. The pink fleshy gums rippled and bubbled as the energy of the spell attempted to wrench everything apart and collapse on itself.

I let a fireball form in the palm of my hands and whipped it down into the darkness of the corrupted dinosaur's throat. The creature opened its mouth, whipping its head back and forth.

The gryphon flew out of the clutches of the creature's sharp teeth. A dino claw swiped through the air right at us. It hit me right in the chest, knocking me off the gryphon. I fell through the air towards the toppled and destroyed ground of Arondale.

The corrupted amalgam turned its focus to the others fighting in the air. It was letting gravity finish me off. Was this it? Was I about to die?

The air rushed through me. My stomach lurched. I swirled in the air and power jumped, hoping to slow my fall. But I fell too fast to balance myself, so it only cushioned my fall for a second. I pivoted at an odd angle towards the approaching ground. I was low on MP—shit, shit, shit. I only had enough mana for one more power jump.

The ruptured pavement and broken houses rushed into view. I infused the bottom of my feet with my last bit of mana and cushioned the fall. Except my depth perception was screwed up and I was still three storeys from the ground. I smashed into the wreckage like an asteroid.

My HP dropped to 5%. A horrible pain ripped through my body. My left leg was covered in blood with a bone poking out of the flesh.

Broken Leg (debuff): *You've broken your leg! Your movement speed decreases by 90%.*

Bleeding (heavy) (debuff): *You have an open wound. You will lose 3 HP every ten seconds. You cannot regenerate health until you stop bleeding.*

Shock (debuff): *You've fallen into a state of shock. Symptoms include blurry vision, nausea, and panic.*

Everything around me was out of focus. I wanted to throw up. I was going to be dead in a minute if I didn't do something. Focus. I took a deep breath. I materialized an HP potion and guzzled it down. By the time I finished it, my vision was back and the shock debuff had disappeared. My leg was still broken and bleeding like crazy though.

I took note of the battle around me. Corpses of Arondale citizens laid crumpled on the ground. Soldiers—including the Royal Knights of Laergard—barked orders and marched down nearby roads in battle squads. All of these people sacrificing their lives to defeat this evil creature and many of them wouldn't ever come back.

The corrupted dinosaur amalgam stared down at me from across the ruined street. It's demonic Skren arm, full of shadows and dark worms, shot out in my direction. It stretched out across the destroyed taverns and houses, overtop the broken ground, the demonic arm mutating new bits of flesh to add to itself so it stretched further and further towards me.

Uh oh.

Instant death here I come.

32

The demonic arm rushed through the air towards my heart. One touch and I'd be dead. It was seconds away from killing me. A bright light flashed. Serena stood blocking the blow, shielding the attack with her giant blade.

The dinosaur recoiled and its arm shriveled back to its regular size. Serena bent down and examined my wounds.

"So you decided to fight a demonic dinosaur without me, huh?"

"Serena," I said, gasping in pain. I still had the broken leg and bleeding debuffs, galloping me towards death. I materialized my MP potion and poured it down my throat. I cast healing mist, focused on my leg. The blood of the wound disappeared and the open flesh of leg stitched up, but the bone was still crooked and broken. I needed a higher-level healing spell to deal with snapped-in-half bones.

"Thanks for saving me," I said. "But I'm pretty useless at the moment."

"Not true," she said. "We're still going to need that ability you unlocked in the dungeon earlier to destroy this thing."

The battle raged in front of us. Kendara circled the creatures head while shooting mana-infused arrows at it. Theobold and Shade swooshed through the air in the hot air balloon shooting magic blasts and bullets. The creature's health had been whittled to 30% HP. Slowly but surely they were destroying the creature.

"They're getting its HP down," said Serena. "We need to get closer for you to unleash your power."

"Um Serena," I said. "I can't move."

"Ridiculous," she said. She slung her blade to her back and bent over and picked me up.

I grinned up at her. "My knight in shining armor."

"Can you shut up for two seconds while we beat this thing?"

Serena jogged across the street with me crumpled in her strong arms. As we got closer, we approached the dinosaurs bottom half. Its humongous legs were each the size of a house.

A voice flickered in my mind as we approached. *Please stop hurting me.*

It was the little girl from my dreams.

The rest of our party kept fighting the creature in the air, attacking its upper body. A barrage of magic, arrows, and bullets punctured the creature's right eye all at once. It wailed in pain. The monstrous scream was enough to make the ground rumble.

"We've almost finished it," yelled Kendara from above. "Everyone blast it with all you got!"

They all attacked ten times harder.

The girl's screams sliced through my mind. What the hell did she want at this moment?

Wait.

Was the corrupted amalgam related to the freaky girl in my dreams? Were the two connected somehow?

The dinosaur swiped its arms in the air as Kendara dodged, swirling in the air on her gryphon. She fired another mana-infused arrow at it. This one shot down right through the creature's throat.

The monster was leaking blood and screaming. It was down to 3% HP.

My wrist ached with pain. The swirling black mark was creeping all over my arm now. It was happening like last time. This power inside me; it was enough to destroy the creature in front of me. I didn't fully understand this power but I knew it would be enough to take the creature out. It wouldn't be able to escape like it had last time. But something about all this wasn't right. Why was I hearing the girl in the heat of battle? Why was she screaming, telling me to stop hurting her? No. I shook my head. It was more of the game's glitches screwing with me, tricking me into not killing it. I had to destroy it: doing so would save Arondale and my friends. There wasn't a real choice here, was there?

"Are you ready Clay?" said Serena, angling my body so I had a clear shot of the creature.

The monster screamed in pain as it dropped to 1% HP.

Here we go.

The power of the mark throbbed through my arm. I needed to unleash it on the beast.

Please... Don't... Do... This...

I lifted my arms. I'm sorry, I said speaking back to it in my thoughts. I have to do

this. To save my friends. To save Arondale. What other choice do I have?

Please.

The swirling black lines ran across my arm. There must

be another way. Destruction wasn't right. I clenched my fingers. *This power has shown me numbers and code before. Show me more. Let's focus on what this power can do.*

The black beam erupted out of my hand and blasted itself at the demonic creature. This time, however, I didn't let the power overwhelm me. I didn't let myself fall unconscious. A whole new set of abilities appeared in my HUD. They were unlike any I'd discovered so far in the game.

//run: virus_scan
//run: fragmentation
//run: defragmentation
//run: restore_corrupted_file
//run: VRmodelling_render

The list went on and on and I focused my eyes on one: "//run: restore_corrupted_file". The dinosaur stopped wailing in pain but relaxed as the blast of power washed over it. I had changed the power from a destructive ability to a curative one. The fragments and worms disappeared off the dinosaur. The blue spirit of the Rorn King evaporated, replaced by a normal dinosaur ribcage. The Skren bandit leader's arm shriveled up and disintegrated into nothing but dust.

A voice echoed in my head, the faintest whisper amongst all the chaos. *Thank you.*

33

The dinosaur returned to its normal self, its stats appearing in my window.

Great Mother Raptor
Level 40
HP: 3 / 2430
MP: 25

It was suffering from a bleeding debuff and the HP dropped further and further until its eyes shut in death. A burst of experience points appeared in my HUD.

The creature wobbled. The shadow of the beast loomed over us and fell in our direction. Serena carried me out of the way as the creature's body collapsed onto the ground, sending one last tremor through the city.

You have successfully completed Quest: Save Arondale!
+3000 EXP!

Congratulations you have leveled up!

You gain +4 HP
You gain +1 MP
You have (3) unused attribute points that can be applied
to any of your five base stats.

"You did it Clay," said Serena, smiling down at me as I hung in her arms.

"This arm. The power, I think, it's—"

We were surrounded by a squad of Royal Knights of Laergard. Their bayonets pointed at us. A prompt appeared in my HUD:

You have lost status with The Royal Knights of Laergard. You have fallen from "Distrusted" status to "Wanted For Suspicious Activity."

Warning: If you descend into further negative alignment, such as "outcast" status, you will no longer be able to enter towns or cities with Royal Knight outposts.

"You're under arrest for the use of forbidden magic," said one of the guards. "Come with us."

A voice yelled, "Stop."

Muscling his way to the front of the crowd was Edward Silver. "This man saved Arondale tonight. He did us a great service. It would be only right to let him go for this evening. If we catch him using forbidden magic again, he'll be bound to us by the law. But tonight, I say we make an exception."

The guards all nodded.

You have gained status with The Royal Knights of Laergard. You have risen from "Wanted for Suspicious Activity" to "Distrusted."

The soldiers dispersed and went to help the injured civilians. Edward Silver gave a curt nod and then hurried away after his soldiers.

Kendara swooshed past on her gryphon and yelled, "I must inform the Aeri of tonight's events. Farewell." She shot off into the distance. She didn't waste any time, did she?

Down the road, Theobold's hot air balloon descended onto the broken cobbled ground. The wizard stepped out of his ship along with Shade. They hurried over to us.

"Well done, Clay," said Shade, bouncing along.

Theobold rushed over to me and waved his hands, casting a spell. A burst of light shot forth from his palm and next thing I knew my leg had been mended, the bone sealed back together.

"Everyone else go off and rest. You," he said pointing a thick gloved finger at me. "Come. We need to talk."

34

"Cover your wrist boy," said Theobold.

We walked through the city streets of Arondale. A few people cheered us as we past, celebrating our heroics. Eventually we ended up in front of the Crow's Heart. We entered and Theobold nodded to Eve, who gave a solemn nod herself. Theobold and I went over and sat in the furthest corner of the pub. Eve brought us over two pints of ale and then left us alone, tending to the other customers at the bar.

"How did you get that mark?" asked Theobold.

I hesitated. What did Theobold want from me? I needed to tell him the truth. I told him about my entry into the game, the fight with the mutant Skren bandit, and the mark it left on my wrist.

"Odd," he said. "Very odd."

"What do you know about the mark?"

Theobold lifted up his right arm and pulled off his glove, revealing a swirling dark mark identical to my own.

"You're not the only one with this curse boy," he said. "There's quite a few of us with such a mark in this world."

"What do you know about it?"

Theobold took a sip of his beer. "I don't even know where or how to begin. I'm sure you've guessed by now. I'm not a normal NPC. I'm a human from Earth, like you. The only difference is I've been living inside A.K.O. for over a decade."

My stomach lurched. "What? The game only launched a week ago?"

The man shook his head, exhausted by his old memories. "I was on the development team. I was a programmer. That's how I know everything I'm about to tell you." He paused to take a sip of his drink. He was trembling. "The game went live roughly twelve years ago internally within TriCorp. Only those on the development team were entering the game on a regular basis. Because there were so few of us in here, we created this dark mark tattoo, as a way of proving to other players we were indeed part of the team. It was a safety precaution. Beyond this—the mark was also important because it was an in-game power used to edit the system. But, as players when we fixed bugs or edited the rendering or architecture of cities, things went awry..."

I fidgeted in my seat, waiting for Theobold to continue.

"You have to understand – once we launched the world and started editing and tinkering with it from the inside, it was very difficult to rewind anything back. We only tinkered with the game at this point. Any mass editing or reprogramming would cause chaos and it did. Those known to have the dark emblem on their wrist were soon viewed by the NPCs as dark gods, reaping destruction on the world. It became known throughout Illyria as a cursed mark."

"Okay," I said, piecing everything he was telling me together. "But you still haven't explained why you've been in here for ten years."

Theobold sighed and continued his long explanation.

"One of the later stages in the development of the game was known as "Realism Testing." Programmers would enter the VR world from the perspective of an NPC, gaining the ability to grant quests and other such things. It was done in an effort to test out quest chains and make sure the NPCs were interacting with each other properly. Or it was the official intention of the testing at least. But upon arriving here in Theobold Longstaff's body, I soon learned I wasn't able to log-out. Konrad Takeshimi had imprisoned me and others in the game. He never explained why. Part of me thinks he's inside here somewhere as well. I've met a few others on the development team but most of us have accepted our lives here. That going home is futile."

This is insane. *Konrad Takeshimi was imprisoning people in here.*

"Theobold—when we were fighting the monster, a young girl came to me in my mind. She's been appearing in my dreams. I think I may have helped her somehow tonight."

"A little girl?" asked Theobold, shocked with disgust. "The mysteries of this game only make you sicker the more you discover them. This game is full of ghosts. The lost consciousnesses of the different people who helped form the system's A.I. I don't know how but you must've created a link with one of them."

The NPCs drinking and chatting across the bar paid no attention to us. Didn't care about whatever human conspiracies we were discussing. They were caught up in their own lives, from personal struggles to the politics of the realm.

What price did Konrad Takeshimi pay to create a world this real?

"That mark on your arm," Theobold continued. "means the internal game system perceives you as a programmer, a developer. You've had dreams and seen fragments of numbers and code, true?"

I nodded my head.

"Those dreams aren't normal dreams. You're seeing the insides of the game's architecture, a place known simply as sub-space. I don't know why you've been granted this power. But I'd be very careful about using it. A.K.O. is unlike any game I've ever experienced, both in terms of play and how it was made and operates. The game's central A.I. is an extremely powerful force and if it catches wind, there are players editing the system yet again, it will react badly. I'd be extremely careful if I were you."

I nodded my head and spoke up: "But Theobold, I don't even know how to use this mark. I've only been able to work it when fighting those mutant creatures and besides—I might not even be here tomorrow…"

Theobold finished his drink and slammed it on the table. "Exactly why we'll continue this conversation *tomorrow*. Right now, you must rest. I don't think it will bode well for Illyria if you were to disappear in the night. I'll be praying to the gods you survive."

The old Rorn mage stood up and walked out of the pub, leaving me sitting at the table alone. The man had given me more questions than answers. I still didn't know why the game was mutating or who the girl talking to me in my dreams was.

I shook my head. I'd have to let these questions go for now.

I stood up, wished Eve good night, and headed up to my bed. The only thing left to do was to go to sleep and dream of a tomorrow.

###PROGRAM: DREAM TRIGGER##

RUNNING DIAGNOSTICS

. . . .

31454390287987083142093187431

I WAS LOST in an ocean of endless white. Was this what Theobold referred to as *sub-space*?

A young girl appeared in front of my eyes. It was the girl from before. Hair tied in brown pigtails. Big circular glasses.

"There are others out there. You need to help them too. Free them like you freed me."

"Who else is out there? Who are you exactly?"

The girl smiled and winked at me. "There's no more time now. The bad one can sense us. We'll talk again soon."

She disappeared abruptly, and I reached out to the blank space where she stood.

"Wait—"

I GASPED AWAKE. The room around me was a blur. My stomach lurched. What the hell is going on? Then I remembered: the battle against the corrupted amalgam, my discussion with Theobold, the cognitive upload. Oh crap—the cognitive upload. I didn't know if I would survive—

Wait.

I was here. In my room at the Crow's Heart Inn. Had I survived the night?

A message appeared in my HUD.

Personal Message: Congratulations!

Congratulations Clay Hopewell on successfully completing the cognitive upload. Your consciousness is now 100% integrated into Arcane Kingdom Online.

Happy adventuring,
TriCorp Dev Team

I had made it through the night. I wobbled out of bed and pulled the cloth blinds, revealing the sunny streets of Arondale. Despite the chaos of the previous evening, the city was back to full swing. Hammers banged and wood sawed as homes and buildings were repaired. The fighting hadn't stopped the merchants from setting up stalls in the market either. Adventurers and travellers were running through the busy streets like they had yesterday. I smiled.

This was officially my new home. I had made it.

A knock banged at my door.

I headed over. Who could that be?

I opened the door and Serena rushed into my arms, hugging me tightly.

"You made it," she said.

She let go of me and closed my door. "I need to talk to you about something. It's urgent. I continued my research last night and—"

A new message popped up in my HUD. It was a universal alert. Serena took a step back, surprised by receiving the sudden message herself.

The message was different from the others I'd received. This one had a window prompt and a play button. I made my HUD press play and a video filled my vision. It was a woman, curly haired, wearing a lab coat with the words TriCorp embroidered on the chest. She was in an office somewhere, speaking into a webcam.

> *"If you receiving this message then things on Earth have truly taken a turn for the worse. The ZERO virus has evolved and spread across the planet. There are not many of us left. The game's much needed patches and updates have not been completed. You'll have to survive within the game as it is currently laid out. This will be the last message you receive from TriCorp or anyone on Earth for a long time. Possibly forever. Be warned—" The developer turned her head to the door. It swung open, revealing a swarm of yellow-eyed creatures. Infected humans with*

*blood stained mouths. They crawled into the laboratory,
drooling. They rushed towards the webcam as the
woman screamed—*

The video cut out.

To Be Continued in...
Arcane Kingdom Online
Book Two!

Author's Note

Thank you for reading my book from start to finish! I hope you enjoyed Clay's adventures in book 1 of Arcane Kingdom Online. If you did, please consider leaving a review. As an indie author, reviews go a long way to achieving success, so please leave one if you can!

If you're craving some more A.K.O. goodness while you wait for Book 2, get a FREE short story set in Illyria by signing up to my mailing list. If you're wondering about that night Shade spent with a Goblin Princess—well, you can hear the whole story by clicking the link below

Join Now!

Thanks again for reading and see you soon!
-Jakob Tanner
www.jakobtanner.com

Join the LitRPG Group on Facebook!

To learn more about LitRPG, talk to authors including myself, and just have an awesome time, please join the LitRPG Group.

Join the GameLit Society for more GameLit and LitRPG!

If you want to hang out with other GameLit fans and authors, consider joining the GameLit Society Facebook group here.

Made in the USA
Columbia, SC
03 March 2021

33868283R00139